WEATHERING *the* FIRESTORM

Inspire Faith, Love, + Hope!

Jen M Hughes

Jen M. Hughes

ISBN 978-1-68526-690-5 (Paperback)
ISBN 978-1-68526-691-2 (Digital)

Covenant Books
11661 Hwy 707
Murrells Inlet, SC 29576
www.covenantbooks.com

1

The fire gained momentum as howling winds and sheets of swirling red-hot embers barreled up the canyon. It was a roaring freight train off the rails. Douglas fir and pine treetops exploded, shooting fireworks into the smoky haze. As the fire leapt from tree crown to tree crown, the blaze became its own entity. A *Dante's Inferno* of destruction with the sole intent to consume everything in its path.

The deafening roar reached Noah Smith before he felt the first searing lick of heat. He snatched the portable radio from his chest harness, then punched the transmit button.

"Attention! This is Chief Smith. Emergency Traffic on Division F. Deploy your shelters immediately. Repeat, deploy your shelters immediately!"

He peered through the thickening billows, assured to find he was the last team member to leave the area. Straining with every muscle fiber, he dug his gloves into the rocky soil to gain enough grip to scale the last few feet of sheer cliff.

As he hoisted himself over the edge, his mind raced. He scanned the area for an open space to deploy his shelter. Perspiration poured down his face as he sought any pathway of escaping certain incineration. He spotted a slight depression on the forest floor. Desperate, he yanked his fire shelter out of his pack and wrestled inside. Once in, he laid as flat as he could, waiting.

The wall of screaming firestorm overtook him. All the moisture was sucked out of his body as the desiccating wall of flame swept over him. Choking and gagging, panic seized him.

I can't breathe!

He pressed into the ground and tugged his bandanna higher, the heat intense, almost intolerable. Frantic, he clung to the edges of the thin shell separating him from death.

As the fire incinerated everything around him, the wind created its own alarming accomplice. Crackling whips and shrieking howls threatening to rip off the shelter. His muscles tensed with the desire to run and flee.

God…please help me… I'm going to burn… I have to run!

No… Stay put…

I'm going to die!

No… It will pass…

Thoughts bounced wildly. Drawing on his years of firefighting training, Noah shut his eyes against the agonizing heat, taking shallow deliberate breaths. Time stood still. He forced himself through sheer determination to wait it out and gritted his teeth as the penetrating heat of the flames became unbearable. Then, as sudden as the firestorm came, it went ravenously seeking more fuel to gorge its insatiable hunger.

While he waited for the winds and blazing embers to calm, he thought of his crew sheltering in place. So many young firefighters, a handful newly married. Many families with young children or expecting. Engineer Dan and his wife were due any day. His yearling firefighter, Josh, was showing lots of potential. Lately, Josh had been coming to work with stars in his eyes from a budding romance with Kat, a new firefighter.

Thoughts of his wife, Ashley, and their two daughters, Emma and Katie, momentarily distracted him. Katie's birthday was tomorrow. His jaw tensed. *I'm going to miss another birthday.* He let out a ragged breath, realizing it was out of his control. The pressing task ahead was to get his crew down the mountain alive.

*****

Ashley slapped at the blaring 6:00 a.m. alarm. Another restless night of tossing and turning. Another day of her first conscious thought being. *How soon can I go back to bed?* She sank into the pillow, reviewing the busy day ahead. Today was Saturday and Katie's tenth birthday. Over a month ago, she had a moment of sheer insanity, agreeing to a pizza party followed by a sleepover for ten of Katie's girlfriends. She'd been powerless against Katie's big brown puppy dog eyes when she'd pleaded to have one friend for each year. After all, she would only turn a full decade once.

Emma had seized on her moment of weakness and somehow convinced her to let two of her friends spend the night as well.

"The more the merrier," she'd told them. *Ha!*

She grimaced, rubbing the sleep from her eyes. *What in the world was I thinking? Twelve twittering tweens plus Emma and Katie?*

She flung her left arm out toward Noah and found the other side of the bed unslept in. Arching her brows, she scooped up her cell phone from the bedside table and swiped for messages. None. Her feet hit the floor.

Noah said he would be home around midnight. He promised he would be released from the fire by 8:00 p.m., report off, and drive straight home. Her heart sank. Katie would be so disappointed if he wasn't here. This was the third birthday in a row he'd missed.

A flash of concern swept through her. *Where was he?* More importantly, *Why hadn't he called or texted?* She chewed her lip nervously and swiped her phone again to double-check. No calls or texts.

Beside her, Trina, their tabby, arched into an exaggerated stretch and delicately yawned before springing from the bed. She meowed at Ashley and swished her tail against her legs.

With a heavy sigh, Ashley shuffled into the bathroom. Persistent dark circles reflected back in the mirror. Turning her body sideways for a profile view, she focused on her thickened middle and love handles. *Well, you are one hot mama!* Her lips curved down into a frown. *I can't imagine why he didn't just run on home like he used to.*

She resolved, starting Monday, to skip the workday Frappuccino with extra whip and go for a brisk walk during her break. Sucking in her tummy, she splashed cold water on her face and brushed her teeth. With a yawn, she shrugged into her robe and cinched the belt snugly around her waist.

Next item on the agenda: coffee—hot, black, and lots of it. Ashley stumbled into the kitchen and flipped on the coffee machine.

She was immediately greeted with joyous barking. As soon as she opened the latch of their two-year-old golden retrievers' crate, brother and sister, Nikki and Callie, bounded out.

"Good morning to you too!" She patted their heads while making her way to the back door.

The dogs fell over each other, leaping out to the backyard and barking wildly at some invisible predator. She shook her head and grinned. Trina called her attention back to the kitchen, meowing mournfully while she pawed at her empty food dish.

Ashley smiled as she refilled her water and spooned out wet food. "So sorry to keep you waiting, Miss Trina."

Trina's tail brushed her ankles as she stepped over her on her way to grab the newspaper from the front porch. She tossed the paper on the kitchen table and filled her mug to the brim. With a grateful sigh, she wrapped her hands around the fragrant steaming brew and sat down. Taking a sip while glancing at the morning headlines, she nearly choked. "On the First Official Day of Fire Season, Will Global Warming Make It a Year-long Event?"

Sputtering, she set down her mug and scrubbed her face with open palms. *Wonderful. Bring it on!*

Anger shot through her body as she flung the newspaper, knocking down their wedding picture. She clasped a hand over her mouth and strode across the room. She stared at the youthful beaming faces looking up at her through the cracked glass. A lump rose in her throat, eyes prickling.

Ashley had prayed to meet her future husband, the man of her dreams. The man God had destined for her from the beginning of time. She prayed to become the woman God intended her to be. She prayed for the family they would have one day and for all the wonderful memories they would create together. Sometimes, it seemed hopeless that the right person would come along, but God's promises in Jeremiah 29:11 often came to her mind.

"For I know of the plans I have for you, declares the Lord, plans to prosper you and not to harm you, plans to give you a hope and a future." Little did she know then, but Noah had been praying this same verse as well. God had a plan for them to be man and wife. A perfect plan.

A decade and a half later, fire season had no beginning or end. It was becoming more difficult to arrange special occasions. Even scheduled days off were often cancelled with no exceptions, except serious hardships. Despite how much Noah loved his job, it wasn't like him not to call if he was able. She tried to reassure herself by thinking about the many justifiable reasons for his delay, which he would explain in his thoughtful and patient way.

He would wrap his arms around her, drawing her in tightly against his muscular chest. His dark brown eyes would gaze hungrily into hers, strong lean biceps locking her body into an ardent embrace. She could almost feel his soft yet firm lips brushing hers, making her feel like she was the only woman on earth.

"*Mom! Mom!*" Katie screamed.

Jolted, she raced up the stairs. "What? Unless there's blood, this better be important."

"Mom," her youngest daughter implored, "Chester's stuck behind the dryer, and he's getting squished!"

"That darned hamster." Ashley wrestled the dryer from the wall. "Did you leave his cage open again?"

She freed the trapped hamster from certain death by dryer and turned to Katie. "Put him in his cage, and make sure you latch the door."

Ignoring her, Katie fussed with Chester and stroked his fur.

Ashley moved the dryer back into position with a stern glance at Katie. "Honey, we have a lot to do before your party, and we're burning daylight. Please go wake up your sister and come downstairs for breakfast. Don't forget, it's your turn to feed the fish. And after breakfast, the dogs need to be walked and Trina brushed."

Katie smiled. "Got it, Mom. Thanks for saving Chester's life!" she added dramatically.

As she headed down the stairs, Ashley called out to her daughter, "You're welcome, and Chester is welcome. But remember to shut his cage from now on."

Back in her bedroom, she glanced at the bedside clock. Another hour had passed with no word from Noah. Chewing her bottom lip, she paced the room. *Something is wrong. I just know it. I feel it.*

2

The roaring thunder of the firestorm passed. Thanking God for His protection, Noah slowly rose out of his locked position, muscles stiff and trembling. The extreme heat slowly dissipated. He shook his arms and head side to side in an attempt to ease the tension. His hands trembled as he grabbed his radio.

"Operations, Division F. We've been burned over. I need air support ASAP." Squinting, he identified a landmark visible from the air. "I'm right at the fire line, mid slope, under Painted Rock."

Rough crackling static came through the receiver before a voice answered, "Operations copies. How many people are in the burn over area?"

"Twenty plus me."

"Operations copies."

"Operations, Air Attack. I have an air tanker and a helicopter I can divert to Division F now."

More static.

"Operations copies: Air Attack, let us know when you have a visual of the area."

"Affirmative."

Noah let out a pent-up breath, knowing help was on the way. Again, he depressed the transmit button. "All personnel on Division F, we will have air support shortly. Stay by your shelters and prepare for a retardant drop."

He radioed a roll call for each member of his division. All twenty were accounted for, and only a few minor burns and scrapes were reported. He sank to his knees. *Thank you, God!*

"Division F, this is Air Attack. We've got a visual on your fire shelters below."

Noah hastily transmitted, "Division F. I can hear you right above us."

"All personnel on Division F, be advised, you'll have a retardant drop over you in about thirty seconds," Air Attack replied tersely.

"Tanker 11, Air Attack. See the Painted Rock outcropping on Division F?"

"Affirmative."

"Tanker 11, be advised there are crews who've deployed shelters in that area. Start your drop just before that rock and follow the contour line, full load at coverage level three."

"Tanker 11 copies. Turning base for short final."

"Tanker 11 turning final. How's my lineup?"

"Good lineup. Clear to drop," Air Attack replied.

Fire retardant rained down all over Noah, speckling his helmet, goggles, and Nomex suit. It was a welcome shower, reducing the stinging heat. Wiping his mouth with his sleeve, he gulped water from his canteen and reflected on what had just happened. Moments before, he was fighting for his life. Now he found himself grinning through a face-full of sticky pink slime.

*****

During Katie's party, Ashley had tried to steer her mind clear of her concern and focus on the event. When asked where Noah was, she had replied lightly, "You know Dad's work. When duty calls, he has to answer." She'd bent down to wrap her arms around Katie's shoulders. "I know he wanted to be here, though."

Katie hung her head. "Wanting to be and actually being here are two different things." She crossed her arms and frowned. "This is the third birthday party he's missed."

"He loves you very much, Katie. If he *could* have been here, he *would* have." Ashley's lips tightened as Katie shrugged dejectedly and rejoined her friends.

All the other times Noah had been delayed and out of contact turned out to be matters beyond his control. This was part of being a firefighter's wife. *Don't let the kids see your concern. Keep things light. You're strong, and you can do this.*

Yet her sense of unease grew stronger.

After the party, Ashley collapsed on the couch in the living room, recovering from a night of nonstop preteen shrieks and hysterical laughter. She'd endured the party without complaint. Her reward was the thankful gleam in her daughter's eyes.

"You are the most awesome mom ever." Katie ran across the room to her mom and snuggled next to her. "All the kids think you're the coolest."

"Thanks, Mom. You're the best. We had so much fun." Emma leaned down to hug her.

The girls chattered happily as they climbed the stairs to their rooms to take a nap. *I'll look back on all this, wishing for these times again.* Exhaustion enveloped her as she unwound streamers from the ceiling fan and picked up paper plates filled with pizza crusts and birthday cake crumbs.

Her fleeting satisfaction disappeared as she checked her phone for the hundredth time. She had yet to hear from Noah. There *must* have been something seriously wrong. In the past, he had always been able to find cell coverage or contact the command center to notify her.

As she cleared the shredded wrapping paper from the coffee table, she happened upon a birthday card from Noah to Katie written several days ago. She lightly ran her fingertips over the words written in his neat block script.

Hi Pumpkin, I love you and wish you a very
Happy Birthday. Dad.

Hot tears flooded her eyes. Too spent to finish the clean-up, she laid on the couch. After falling into a sound, dreamless sleep, she was startled by the sound of the front doorknob turning.

The instant she saw Noah, any angry accusations fell silent. His uniform was torn and filthy. Dirty black smudges of soot streaked his face. His eyebrows and lashes were singed, face reddened and raw. Black circles ringed his bloodshot eyes.

"Oh!" She rushed over to him, searching his face. "What happened? Are you all right?"

He pulled her against him. "Babe, I'm so sorry I missed Katie's party. The fire flared up when the winds came. We were caught in a canyon and had to deploy our shelters. It was blowing and going in rugged terrain. I had no cell phone coverage. Our division had to stay on the fire throughout the night to watch for flare-ups. The Incident Commander wouldn't release anyone until relief crew arrived this morning." He gripped her shoulders and looked into her eyes. "I wanted to be here for you and the girls. Will you forgive me?"

Cupping his face, she brushed his dry, parched lips with a soft kiss. "Of course we forgive you. Thank God you're alive! Is everyone else all right?"

He nodded, the weathered lines on his forehead furrowing. "Yes. A few scrapes, couple cases of heat exhaustion, and minor burns. The air tanker drops did an amazing job." He stepped back and rolled his shoulders. "Oh, it's so amazing to be home." With a glance around the room, he clapped his hands together. "Listen. The least I can do is clean up. You look exhausted. I want to do my part." He rubbed the middle of her back. "Go take a nap. I'll handle this."

"*No way!* Are you kidding? This is nothing compared to what you've been through! I have a better idea." She smiled coyly. "Why don't you shower? Then we'll snuggle. Let this wait till later."

Noah grinned back, raising his eyebrows. "You always have the best ideas!"

As they set off down the hallway, their beloved kitty Trina padded behind.

Later, Noah drifted off to sleep. Listening to his snores, Ashley was thankful he was beside her. She unwrapped herself from his arms as she twisted and fretted the fears, concerns, and doubts about being a firefighter's wife plagued her until she fell into a fitful sleep.

3

The workweek started with a bang. Several nurses called in sick with the flu. As the day shift charge nurse in the forty-bed Level III Neonatal Intensive Care Unit, it was Ashley's responsibility to find replacements. After placing a dozen calls, she was able to find several recent nursing school graduates eager to work a day shift for a change and who could use the extra overtime pay.

In the break room for a ten-minute reprieve, she heated water in the microwave and plopped in an Earl Grey tea bag. With a grateful sigh, she sat down. She remembered those days early in their marriage, both of them jumped at overtime shifts when the opportunity arose.

It took two years, but with both of them working long, hard shifts, they finally earned the down payment for their house. Content, they painted, replaced flooring, and made it their own.

One year later, Emma was born followed two years later by Katie. The household grew as their kitty Trina was added to the family. A year ago, they brought home Nikki and Callie, two adorable little fur balls who were small enough to sit in each girl's lap.

Ashley glanced up at the clock. Time to head back to work.

Dr. Cook, the NICU medical director, waved her over when she entered the unit. He cupped his other hand over the phone receiver. "I'm talking to Dr. Chan about transporting twenty-four-week gestation twins. No prenatal care, no other history. Mom showed up at the ER with one of the twins' head crowning. Apgar scores were very low. They're hand-bagging both babies, ventilating with 100 percent oxygen, and their vital signs are unstable. The hospital doesn't have the equipment or staff to take care of them. We need to send a transport team STAT. Is it possible for you to put together a double team and set up for the fixed wing aircraft to transport?"

Ashley rubbed the back of her neck. "Well, we currently have four beds available. Team One has already been dispatched and are on their way back. Team Two is en route. If you need a transport STAT, I could probably go with Nick. We could ask Laurie and Mark if they could assist as back-up for the twins."

"Thank you, Ashley. I knew I could count on you to pull a plan together." Dr. Cook squeezed her shoulder. "Butte Hospital is small and remote. The staff isn't familiar with extreme prematurity, so the sooner you can get there, the better chance these babies will have."

"Consider it done! I'll let you know our ETA once we get airborne." Heading to the room where the transport Isolettes were stored, she put in a quick call to Noah to let him know what was going on. His cell went to voice-mail, so she left a message.

"Hi, babe. It's me. It's about 1:00, and I need to do a STAT transport for twins. I might be delayed, so please pick up the girls from school. Call me back when you get a chance. If I don't answer, I'm busy, so leave a message. Love you!"

She felt apprehensive about heading off to predictably a long transport without speaking to Noah. Hopefully, he was off-duty and able to pick up the girls. Nick and Ashley prepped for the transport, checking off the itemized list. When they finished, they waited in the corridor for the ambulance to take them to the airport.

As the ambulance pulled up, Nick glanced over with a smile. "Did you realize it's been almost two decades since we graduated from college together?"

"Time flies when you're having fun," she quipped.

Nick groaned. "All those long twelve-hour night shifts."

"We were so wet behind the ears."

"Babies ourselves!" he smiled.

"Now look at us. All grown up with kids and mortgages."

"There's no one else I would rather go on transport with. Much respect." Ashley made a fist over her heart and flashed a grin at Nick.

"Thanks. I feel the same."

The transport incubator, equipped with every life support piece of equipment available, was loaded onto the ambulance. Upon arriving at the airport. It was loaded into the twin-engine fixed-wing aircraft specially fitted for the transport incubator and two team members.

Ashley checked her cell phone for messages from Noah. There weren't any. "Doggone it!"

"What's up?" Nick inquired.

"Oh. I left a message asking Noah to pick up the girls from school in half an hour, and he hasn't answered back yet." She held her palms up in exasperation. "I don't know if he got tied up at work or not. I just hate not knowing. What am I supposed to do? I have a job to do as well!"

Nick paused then spoke, "I'm sure Jackie would be happy to get Emma and Katie. You know our kids love hanging out with them. She can swing by their school after picking our kids up. They can even spend the night, and she can take them to school in the morning. They'll have a blast."

Ashley squeezed his hand. "You're a true friend. What would I do without you and Jackie?"

"You got it." Nick pulled out his cell and called his wife.

After they chatted for a few minutes, Ashley gestured for him to hand her the phone. "Jackie, I can't thank you enough."

"No worries," she said. "We love having Emma and Katie over. They're such sweet girls, and the kids will be excited to have friends over. Now don't worry about anything. Just take care of those little babies! I'm heading over to their school, and then we'll come home, have a snack, and do homework."

"You're an angel! Please give the girls a big hug and kiss for me and tell them either Noah or I will be home as soon as possible. I'll call the school right now to let them know you will be picking them up."

Now that she knew the girls were in good hands, she could focus on the important job ahead. She sent a quick text to tell Noah the change of plans and settled in for the flight, ticking off in her head the sequence for stabilizing the twins when they arrived at the hospital.

As the plane landed at the airport, Ashley and Nick double-checked their equipment and radioed the hospital of their imminent arrival. They were met by an ambulance which took them swiftly to the hospital with lights flashing and sirens blaring Code Three. Not a moment too soon, they arrived at the labor/delivery unit. The twin babies, a boy and girl, each weighed less than two pounds. Their lungs, hearts, and all other vital systems weren't yet mature enough to support life. When the transport team arrived in the delivery room, the local staff was making a valiant effort to insert the necessary umbilical artery catheters and stabilize the infants' breathing and blood pressure.

Ashley quickly assessed the preemies with an experienced eye. Coordinating care closely with Nick, she verbalized her assessment. "Both of their blood pressures are dropping. I'm going to administer twenty milliliters of fresh frozen plasma slow IV push to them. Afterward, I'm going to set up a Dopamine drip titrated to maintain their blood pressure."

Nick studied the monitor and shook his head. "Their carbon dioxide levels are way too high. They're both compensating but running out of steam. Ashley, can you assist me while I insert breathing tubes? Then we'll get an arterial blood gas and see where we're at."

As Ashley and Nick worked diligently over the twins, they were joined by their backup team, Laurie and Mark, who had arrived on a second flight and ambulance drive to the hospital. They had brought a second transport Isolette. Ashley turned and flashed a smile of relief. "Thank goodness you guys are here. We really need another pair of hands!"

Both teams worked together in a practiced, efficient manner, using their expertise to maximize the micro-preemies chances of survival. After several hours of intensive nursing care, assisted by the skill of the experienced respiratory therapists, both of the babies were stabilized enough to be moved into the transport Isolettes.

While Ashley relayed the status of the infants to Dr. Cook back at the NICU, Laurie confirmed the arrangements for the ambulance to take them back to the airport for the return flight. She also alerted the acting charge nurse of their status and ETA. When these details were attended to, Ashley and Laurie had several minutes to catch up on each other's busy lives.

"So how have you been coping with fire season?" Laurie asked.

The pair of them went back many years, having gone to nursing school together. Both of them started their nursing careers in the NICU. Laurie and her firefighter husband David had introduced Ashley and Noah on a blind date, which led to a whirlwind romance and marriage within a year. Ten years ago, Laurie had delivered premature twin boys, and they also had an older daughter. She was very familiar with the challenges of being a firefighter's wife.

"It's been tough." Ashley grimaced. "I love him. But where does my life and our life fit in?" She met Laurie's gaze. "Just this past weekend, he was stuck on a fire, almost killed in a burn over, and missed Katie's tenth birthday party." Her shoulders drooped. "This is the third birthday party in a row he's missed." She raised her voice in frustration. "Today I couldn't even reach him when I was asked to do this transport. He was supposed to be off duty this morning."

"It's tough being a firefighter's wife." Laurie pulled her in for a quick hug.

"Thankfully, Jackie picked them up." Exasperated and tired, Ashley chewed her lip. "Why am *I* always the one worrying about our children and making sure they're being taken care of?" Tears filled her eyes. "I'm just getting a little tired of his work taking precedence over mine and our family."

Her voice cracked. "I love him so much, Laurie, but this is really getting to me!"

"I understand where you're coming from. David and I have had more than one disagreement about the same problem. I was as frustrated as you sound." She gave her friend a hug and then put both hands squarely on Ashley's shoulders. "Frankly, it came down to a separation and almost divorce, which neither of us really wanted. It's better now since I cut back to part-time.

"Also, since David has been promoted to division chief, his hours are more stable. It's rough, I know, and it sounds likes this is going to be a crazy fire season!" She gave Ashley's shoulder a squeeze. "I'm here for you any time you need to talk or vent. Remember that."

The ambulance drove up to take them to the waiting aircraft for the flight back to the NICU. Ashley allowed herself a deep sigh of exhaustion, releasing nervous tension from the previous hours of intense concentration. She wouldn't rest until the twins were safely transported to the NICU and her own precious daughters were nestled in their beds at home.

Jackie and Nick's offer for the girls to spend the night was appreciated, but it was a school night. By the time she got off-duty, it would be around 7:00 p.m. Ashley would pick up the girls, oversee their baths, and tuck them into bed. After they were settled in, she would grab some leftovers for dinner. Tomorrow was another work day, and there were several meetings, including a monthly staff meeting for which she still needed to prepare the agenda.

She glanced at her phone. Still no messages. Taking one more deep cleansing breath, she rolled her shoulders and climbed aboard the airplane for the flight back.

Thirty-five minutes later, they landed safely and loaded the transport Isolettes into the waiting ambulance. After a short trip back to the hospital, the twins were settled in their waiting Isolettes and report was given to the shift charge nurse. Relieved of her duties, she again checked her cell phone and saw a voice mail message from Noah.

"Hi, honey. I just got your message. We were dispatched right before change of shift to a brush fire. Four homes burned, and the area was evacuated. I'm sorry I couldn't pick up the girls or call you sooner. It was pretty intense. There wasn't any cell coverage. The fire is only about 5 percent contained, so I don't know when I'll be home. I'll keep you updated when I can. Love you!"

Ashley was beyond exhausted by the time she tucked Emma and Katie in for the night with bedtime prayers and kisses. Too tired to even think, she mindlessly prepared the coffee maker for the morning and packed lunches. She set the alarm for 6:00 a.m. With a sigh, she glanced over at the empty pillow.

4

The sun rose over the horizon like an enormous red ball. Smoke from the nearby wildfire drifted over the area, casting a dirty haze in the neighboring skies. *Bad sign.* Ashley hurried down the driveway and stooped to pick up the morning paper. The air felt static and dirty. She glanced at the outdoor thermometer. At 7:00 a.m., it was already seventy-five degrees! They were in for another scorcher. Weather forecasts were predicting a high of 102 with very little humidity.

Of more concern than the heat or the humidity was the fact that north winds were predicted to increase in the afternoon. Emma and Katie clambered into the car as she scanned the skies again.

After dropping off the girls at school, Ashley began the long commute to work, her hands tense on the wheel as ominous dark gray clouds built up in the distance. From years of being married to a firefighter, she knew these were not rain clouds but smoke from the fire.

These massive billows of smoke were called headers. They looked like a threatening thunderstorm but were caused by the fire consuming enormous amounts of vegetation. Wildfires were notorious for creating their own weather patterns with erratic winds, even fire tornadoes. Widow-makers, Noah called them. Shivering, she brushed back the raised hairs on her arms.

Scowling at the gigantic header, she turned on the car radio to catch the morning news just as the announcer was giving an update on the fire Noah was assigned to. He confirmed Ashley's earlier assessment of the weather.

"Increases in inland pressure are bringing in above-average seasonal temperatures and desiccating north winds overnight, causing the fire to break through containment lines. Several homes have been totally destroyed, and many more are now under threat. The fire is currently estimated to be only ten percent contained and has consumed over five thousand acres."

Ashley's eyes widened. Her hands tightened around the steering wheel as the broadcast continued.

"Red flag conditions are in effect through Tuesday afternoon for severe fire weather. The combination of high temperatures, strong winds, and low humidity are the perfect mix for some of the worst and most destructive fires we've seen in a decade."

This was her greatest fear. She tapped her nail on the wheel. It was going to be a long dangerous fire season. She made a mental note to reach out to the other firefighter wives as she entered the hospital parking lot.

The announcer made one last plea to the listeners. "Please be careful out there, folks. You know the drill: no campfires and no activities that could ignite a fire. Electricity and gas shutoffs are very likely, so be prepared."

Ashley turned off the radio. She had heard enough to realize there was no chance Noah would be home today or any day soon. Fire season was in full effect. She missed the life they had before fire season had gotten so out of control and wished for the times when they could plan a date night or even a family getaway. Now their time together was practically nonexistent.

Noah grounded Ashley. He kept her from being stuck in her head, worrying, trying to take on everything, especially things that were out of her control. She closed her eyes and locked on to a memory from early in their marriage when she was working long hours. He had rubbed her shoulders with his adept fingers, easing the tight knots of tension, and bent down to whisper, "Take good care of yourself. You belong to me."

She pulled into an employee parking spot then gathered her purse and tote bag. At least her shift wouldn't be as long as yesterday's. Unless something had changed since last night, NICU beds were at full capacity. They were closed to transports until a bed opened up.

However, she did have a full schedule of staff meetings and other responsibilities to attend to, which would very quickly fill her day.

As she walked to the entrance and swiped her ID, she greeted the security guard. "Hey, Rodney. How's the family? Is your little guy feeling better?"

He smiled. "Morning, Ashley. Yeah, he's doing okay now. Just had a bad ear infection but feeling better after a couple of days on antibiotics."

"Good news! Now everyone can get some rest."

"Thanks. You have a good one."

"You too."

She hung her purse on a locker hook and grabbed her lab coat. After putting it on, she clipped on her name tag and swung her stethoscope around her neck. She filled her front pocket with work essentials, and turned for the break room.

After opening the staff fridge, she shuffled items around to make space for her lunch. She noticed many items were well past their expiration dates. Another item on the staff meeting agenda: *Clean your items out of the fridge daily to allow room for everyone's food.*

Greeting coworkers with a nod and smile, she strode down the hallway, then stepped into her office to quickly check messages and e-mail before her morning rounds. Another busy day in the NICU was up and running. Before she knew it, the day had breezed by in a whirl. Waving goodbye to the ever-watchful Rodney, she headed out to her car.

It was Wednesday. Both girls had horseback riding lessons after school. She looked forward to picking them up from school and taking them to the barn. Ashley was raised in the suburbs but enjoyed the friendly country atmosphere of the riding stable. It was peaceful and relaxing to sit in the shade of a tree while watching graceful horses and smelling the fresh alfalfa.

Spotting Emma and Katie in the pick-up line, she sent a cheery wave. The girls clambered into the car and fastened their seat belts, eager to share their day.

"I got an A on my spelling test," Katie announced proudly.

"Two boys got into a fight at lunch, and they both got suspended. Everybody crowded around, but I didn't," Emma confided. "I don't like fighting. It makes me sad to see people hurt each other."

Katie jumped into the conversation, "I heard the boys were fighting over you, Emma. They both like you."

"They do not! Stupid boys." Emma flung her long blonde hair aside and crossed her arms.

"Emma has a boyfriend," Katie taunted. "Two boyfriends, in fact."

"I do not."

"Okay, girls, settle down now. We're going to have a nice afternoon at the barn. No arguing or teasing allowed."

Katie turned to her sister. "Sorry, Emma, but I did hear that both boys like you."

"Apology accepted. But even if they like me, it doesn't mean I like them. They're dumb."

"Change of topic," Ashley ordered. "If you're hungry, there are protein bars and fruit in the cooler with your waters. Be sure to get hydrated before your lessons."

This was a highlight of the week for both girls. Emma had ridden for four years now, and Katie two. Both had an affinity for animals, but Katie, in particular, was horse crazy. Her bookshelf at home was lined with horse books. Walls were covered with pictures of her favorite horses and their famous riders. The girls spent long hours playing with their horse figures, setting up mini barns and corrals. Katie had shown her innate riding talent at an early age. After watching hours of the summer equestrian Olympics, she had decided that when she grew up, she was going to be an Olympic show jumper.

When they arrived at the stable, Emma and Katie headed into the barn. The whiteboard announced Emma would be in the intermediate class in ring three on Sammy. Katie would be riding Sadie, a seasoned school horse, in ring one with the beginner riders. Chatting with their barn friends, they brushed and tacked up, carefully checking their horses' feet for stones before saddling. Emma took the lead, walking her horse to ring three while Katie followed and entered ring one. The group lessons began with each rider warming up their horses, first walking then trotting. Once the horse was warmed up, they moved into a canter.

"Mom, Mom, look at me!" Katie fearlessly sailed over eighteen-inch crossbars with a delighted grin.

"Great job! Go around again, and I'll video it so you can watch later."

"Okay!" Katie pressed her heels into the horse's side, encouraging him to circle around.

While Katie cooled down her horse after the lesson, Ashley looked around for Emma and spotted her chatting with some other kids.

"Hey, Mom, this is Olivia and Charlotte. They're twin sisters in my grade and just joined the barn."

"Hi! Are you new to riding?"

"No, we've been taking lessons now for a few years. Our family just moved here from the East Coast. We go to the same school as Emma, just in another class," Olivia said.

"Olivia and Charlotte take jazz classes at Dance Company, that new studio around the corner from the school," Emma enthused.

"Yeah, the teachers are great, and we can walk there after school. It would be fun if Emma could join us." Charlotte smiled and clasped her hands.

"Please, Mom?" Emma gave her an engaging grin. "Please? It's what I have been wanting to do forever."

"Sounds interesting. We'll check into it and discuss it with Dad." Ashley wrapped her arm around Emma's shoulder.

As they walked to the car, the girls shared highlights of their lesson.

"I jumped an eighteen-inch crossbar," Katie beamed.

"That's great. I did a two-foot triple jump but knocked over a couple rails."

"What's for dinner? I'm starving."

Emma threw her boots and hat in the back seat as she climbed into the SUV. "Me too. When's Daddy coming home?"

Ashley looked up the setting sun, a red ball in the smoke-filled sky. "I wish I knew, honey. From the look of things not anytime soon." Turning on the ignition, she plastered on a smile and glanced in the rearview mirror. "How does grilled chicken and mashed potatoes sound? We have some left-over salad from last night too."

"Yummy." Katie clapped her hands.

"Can we have garlic bread too? I'll help," Emma offered.

"Me too," Katie jumped in. "I'll feed the dogs and Trina."

Putting the car in drive, she took in a deep breath. "Teamwork. Love it." Taking another glance at the vibrant sunset, she steeled herself for what looked like a long haul.

5

Things weren't looking hopeful for Noah to be released anytime in the near future. Conditions were perfect for this year to win the distinction of being the most devastating fire season on record. Every time one fire broke out, several more followed. As soon as one was contained and personnel were released, they were sent to the next fire. Mandatory staffing patterns were in effect, meaning everyone was held on duty with no days off, and approved scheduled vacations were cancelled.

Noah placed a quick call to Ashley. The phone rang until the familiar voice-mail message played.

"Hey, Ashley. It's me. Sorry I've been out of touch. Cell coverage is spotty. Just calling to say I love you. This fire is out of control. Maybe you've been following it on the news. We've just been advised mandatory staffing patterns are on...so no days off. I'm doing all right, just tired. Missing my girls and hope everything is okay. Love you."

The fire service was a call to duty similar to the armed forces. With people's lives and property at stake, this was serious. The governor had just declared a state of emergency in several counties. Numerous communities were under mandatory evacuations, and several others had voluntary evacuations strongly recommended.

People were resistant to evacuations. They were afraid of losing their possessions, thinking if they stayed, they could protect their homes. That decision often resulted in disaster. In addition to property, lives were lost. He missed his family, but this was what he was called to do. People counted on him, and he was not going to fail them or his crew.

*****

Ashley's schedule was filled with committee meetings and potential new employee interviews on top of her regular duties. She was constantly having to put out fires of her own. She loved her job as a nurse, but recently, the administration portion of her position was taking over her real love of bedside nursing. Over the past few years, there'd been a significant shift toward hospital administrators becoming more business-oriented and less patient-oriented.

The almighty dollar seemed to rule the world. Several of the charge nurse positions had been reassigned as manager positions and had been filled with people who had business degrees, not nursing degrees. This was creating major problems as these individuals lacked understanding of what bedside nursing entailed.

A prime example of this was a meeting she had attended earlier that day. The hospital administrator had called a mandatory all-staff supervisors meeting.

Mr. Jensen, the hospital administrator, stood arrogantly at the podium in front of a large screen. The PowerPoint presentation was entitled "Time Studies."

"The purpose of this meeting is to inform you that the hospital board has hired a firm to monitor each bedside nurse for one week."

Ashley fought the urge to roll her eyes. *What a ridiculous waste of time and financial resources.*

"They will be timing individual nursing functions for effectiveness of movement. At the end of the study, the results will be compiled and discussed." He peered around the room with a commanding authority as if daring anyone to question him.

Then what? Nurse A took forty-five seconds to soothe a crying child. This could have been done as effectively in forty seconds. Or Nurse B took thirty seconds too long administering medications. It was absolutely ridiculous and an insult to the nursing profession. How could someone who had no clue of what was involved with the intricate details of nursing, especially caring for neonatal and pediatric patients, determine how long a procedure should or should not take? Ashley noted other nursing supervisors shaking their heads and frowning.

When the administrator finished his lengthy tirade, the moderator opened the floor for questions and comments.

Ashley couldn't hold back any longer. Face flushed, she boldly raised her hand.

The moderator nodded his head in her direction. "Yes." He glanced down at her badge. "Nurse Smith, please come to the mic so we can all hear you."

She cleared her throat as she stood and wiped her sweaty palms on her jacket. "I have a question and a comment."

"Please go ahead."

"How does one determine how long it should take to soothe a crying child?" she asked.

The moderator looked at her with a puzzled expression. "Excuse me?"

Taking a deep breath, Ashley forged ahead. "It seems to me that nurses should be the ones evaluating how long a nursing function should take. Not a stopwatch." She glanced around the room. Many of her colleagues were grinning, several with their thumbs up in support. She pressed forward, grabbed the mic, and raised her voice, emphasizing each word. "How does someone *measure* whether administrating a medication should take one minute or two? The most important thing is not how long it takes but that the *right* medication in the *right* dosage at the *right* time to the *right* patient and *right* route is administered. That is called the five rights of medication administration. It is an important skilled nursing intervention and the leading cause of hospital errors. Nursing functions are taught, trained, take experience, and should *not* be timed events." Ashley's cheeks bloomed hot. "We are *humans* taking care of other *humans! Not robots!*"

She strode back to her seat, noting most of her coworkers nodding their heads firmly. Many clapped in support. Several others gave her high fives or thumbs up.

"Thank you for your comments," the moderator replied.

The hospital administrator glared at her from across the room as the moderator continued, "Any other comments or questions?"

One after another, the supervisors approached the mic and concurred with Ashley's remarks.

At the end of the comments, Mr. Jensen held up his hand. "I have a final comment. While each of you have the right to an opinion, your opinions do not change the fact that the time study is not optional."

Amid complaints and a few boos, he stalked out of the room, ending the meeting. Negative comments filtered throughout the room in his wake.

"Since he arrived last year, morale has gone downhill fast."

"Yeah, it's like the saying, 'The beatings will continue until morale improves.'"

"What a jerk. I'm dreading telling my staff about this. There's already been rumbling that some nurses have been interviewing at other hospitals because of him and his management style."

Ashley fumed as she strode down the hallway to the NICU. Deep in thought, she accidentally bumped into the person walking in front of her. She quickly apologized and attempted to walk around him.

"Ashley! Hey, I thought that was you. I haven't seen you in ages. How's it going?"

Momentarily stunned, she stepped backward. "Steve?" she questioned, voice faltering. Ashley pulled her thoughts away from the previous meeting to focus on the person greeting her with a friendly smile. Even after all these years, she recognized his gorgeous turquoise eyes and handsome face immediately.

"Steve! So good to see you. What are you doing here? The last I heard, you were living in LA." She gave him a quick friendly hug and stepped back to study him. The years had been kind to her former boyfriend.

6

Steve flashed his perfect white teeth, eyes twinkling as he smiled. "It's so great to see you!"

She smiled back and inquired. "What brings you here?"

"I'm in town for a few days, attending a seminar and networking. The cardiology staff invited me to demonstrate a new surgical procedure I use to repair congenital cardiac defects. We've been having a lot of success with the procedure in LA."

Ashley nodded with appreciation. "That's awesome. I'm hearing some fascinating things about your work. Are your wife and family in town with you? It would be fun if you could all come to dinner. The girls would love to meet your daughters. I think they're about the same ages. Noah is on a fire, but I would enjoy cooking and catching up on what's been going on."

Steve grinned. "That sounds wonderful. I'm more than a little tired of all the chicken and rice dishes they tend to serve at these dinner meetings." A shadow cast over his attractive face. "Unfortunately, it's just me. Stephanie and I divorced two years ago. She has primary custody of Cara and Lexie since I'm out of town so much, but the girls are usually at my place one or two times a week when I'm home."

"I'm sorry. You had mentioned before that you and Stephanie were having a tough time, but I was hoping it would work out."

"We tried," he said with a sad smile. "My long hours at work, in addition to all the traveling I do, was too much for Stephanie. She liked the idea of being married to a doctor but not the lifestyle the job required." He raised his hands in a "*Go figure*" expression. "At least we're still on friendly terms. I try to hold up my end financially and spend as much time as I possibly can with the kids."

"I can relate to that. Noah's job takes him away all the time, and it does get old after a while." She waved her hands to brush away the topic. "Anyway, let's not dwell on that. How does tomorrow night at seven work for you?"

"That sounds perfect. I look forward to visiting with you and having a home-cooked meal for a change."

"Is chicken and rice okay?" She laughed at Steve's perplexed face. "I'm kidding. I promise, no chicken and no rice."

His face creased into a boyish smile. "You got me. See you tomorrow at seven."

They exchanged contact information, and Ashley slipped her phone back in her pocket. "I'll text the address. Call if you need directions." She sent a jaunty wave as she continued down the hospital corridor.

*****

Ashley and Steve had met many years ago when they both worked at the hospital. They dated for several years when she was in nursing school and Steve worked in the cardiac procedure's lab while taking premed classes. They shared a love of hiking and kayaking. Often, on a hot summer night after work, they would grab a picnic dinner and head out to the local lake. Paddling their kayaks, they'd stop at a sandy point to eat their picnic dinner and swim. Laying their towels on the warm sand, they would watch the sunset, sharing dreams and plans for the future.

Steve hoped to one day become a pediatric cardiologist. Ashley had a heart for pediatrics, specifically neonatal ICU. It was her dream to work as an RN in the NICU and be a transport nurse. Little did they know than that both of their career dreams would come true... just not together.

One night, Steve took her out to their favorite restaurant and asked her to marry him. As much as she loved him, she knew they needed to stay focused on school and establishing their careers.

He promised to ask her again after graduation, but time and distance slowly pulled them apart. Ashley knew God had something different and better in store for each of them.

Parting with assurances to stay in touch, they each went their separate ways. Ashley flew down to LA. Steve came up to visit as often as he could. Their reunions were joyful and full of promises to see each other soon. However, medical school and nursing school were full-time commitments in addition to their jobs.

As with most long-distance relationships, time and distance slowly pulled them apart.

7

"Hi, babe! How are you? I miss you." Noah's voice sounded tired and rough.

"I'm fine. Let me put you on speaker. I'm cooking dinner." Touching the speaker button, Ashley began layering the lasagna. "The girls are doing well too. They're upstairs finishing homework before our dinner guest comes. Hey, I saw the huge fire header on my way to work. That thing was massive."

Noah cleared his throat. "Just a sec. My throat is parched." He coughed and gulped some water. "Yep. The fire is blowing and going. It's gonna be a long road, I'm afraid. Lots of evacuations, and we're short on resources."

"Please take care of yourself. You sound dehydrated and exhausted. Are you taking those electrolyte tablets I gave you?"

"Thanks for the reminder. I'll pop a couple in my water bottle right now."

She heard him rummage in his bag, followed by the plop and fizz when he added the tablets to his water. "Who's the dinner guest?"

Ashley covered the pan with foil and slid it into the oven. "Remember Steve Walker? He's an old friend of mine who's a pediatric cardiologist living in LA. I ran into him at the hospital and invited him for dinner. He's in town for a few days and looked like he could use a home-cooked meal. I'm making lasagna. Carrot cake for dessert."

Noah cleared his throat again. "Just Steve? What about his wife and kids?"

"Only Steve." Ashley set the timer. "He and his wife divorced two years ago. His career and long separations didn't work out for them. He's settled now in LA, doing some cutting-edge procedures for pediatric patients with congenital heart disease. That's why he's in town, teaching the procedure to our doctors. Really incredible work, saving children's lives who had no chance at all before his discovery." She pulled out the cream cheese frosting she had prepared earlier and dug a big dollop to frost the cake. "Are you still there?"

Noah took a ragged breath. "Sorry to hear about their divorce. Well, tell him I said hi. I wish I was there to enjoy your company… and lasagna."

"Me too! Noah, did you remember our fifteenth anniversary is coming up in two weeks? We have some very special plans. You *are* still approved for vacation time, right?"

"I can't wait to celebrate our anniversary. I miss us. As far as I've been told, my time off is approved. However, there is talk about mandatory staffing patterns."

"I miss us too." Ashley wished she could put her arms around him and lean on his strong shoulders. She needed him, his touch, and his security.

He blew out a long weary breath. "I love you all so much, and I'm so sorry I wasn't available to pick up the girls and caused you extra stress."

"It all worked out thanks to Jackie stepping up to help with the girls. We all love you and just want you home safely with us. Let's pray the winds die down." Concern furrowed her brow. "You sound beyond tired. Get some rest. Be safe. I love you."

*****

"Wow, that smells amazing!" Steve took off his jacket and handed Ashley a pretty bouquet. "A small gift. It's been so long since I had a home-cooked meal I can't even remember when."

Taking the gift with a smile, Ashley motioned toward the family room. "Please make yourself comfortable. Give me a sec, and I'll put these in a vase, then we can catch up before dinner's ready. Can I get you something to drink? Water? Herbal tea?"

"Water would be great. Thanks."

She called up the stairs. "Emma, Katie! Come downstairs and say hi to Steve."

The girls clambered down the stairs, followed by their two golden retrievers and cat eager to sniff out the new arrival.

"This is Emma, our oldest, and Katie. Girls, this is Steve. We went to college together many years ago. He has two daughters the same ages as you and is a pediatric cardiologist visiting from LA."

"Oh, that's cool. Their hearts must be so little." Emma made a little heart shape with her fingers.

Steve chuckled and made a smaller heart shape. "Some are even smaller...like this. Tell me about your furry friends here."

Katie was eagerly talking about the animals when Ashley went to check on dinner. "Be right back."

They had about thirty minutes before it was ready. *Perfect timing.* She filled up two tumblers with cool water. Handing a glass to Steve, she smiled at the motley collection of children and animals all vying for his attention.

"Come have a seat." He patted the couch next to him. "You've been working all day and now making dinner. Your wonderful daughters are telling me all about your household menagerie and their riding lessons. Emma tells me she may be starting jazz dance lessons soon."

"We've been talking about it. I just need to discuss it with Noah first." She glanced at her watch. "Girls, we have about a half hour before dinner. Why don't you go finish your homework?"

After the girls went back upstairs, Ashley and Steve chatted, catching up on each other's lives. Ashley relaxed, enjoying having some adult conversation at the end of the day. *I miss this. It's lonely without a companion and partner. It seems as if Noah's gone far more than he's home.*

As she studied Steve's striking profile, she remembered why she had been attracted to him many years ago. He had the toned look of an athlete. His eyes were aquamarine with dark, thick lashes, and when he smiled, cute little dimples appeared on his cheeks.

We used to have a lot of fun together.

Steve was also somewhat of a daredevil. Their dates were often adventuresome group treks going backpacking or skiing. He had a wonderfully relaxed manner and was a great travel companion. He was an all-around terrific guy and smoking hot.

Whoa, girl! You need to get off that train of thought right now. You are a happily married woman who is missing her husband—who also happens to be a very handsome and terrific guy.

In an attempt to refocus, she stood up. "I'm going to finish the dinner preparations. The remote is next to you if you want to watch the news or there are some magazines on the side table."

Steve immediately stood. "Or I could help you in the kitchen if that's okay."

"Sure, but you don't have to."

"I want to."

"All right, why don't you finish up the salad? All the vegetables and salad fixings are in the right-hand drawer of the fridge."

Several hours later, Ashley walked Steve to the door.

He smiled down at her and gave her a friendly hug. "It was so great seeing you. Thank you for a fantastic dinner. It was truly outstanding. I loved visiting with the girls and all the members of your animal family. It was an oasis from my normal routine of fast food or those awful chicken and rice banquets. Noah is a lucky man."

"Thank you."

"Please stay in touch and contact me if you're ever in the LA area. I would love to return the favor."

"I will. Best of luck with all the tremendous work you're doing. Maybe our family can come down sometime." She tapped her chin with her index finger. "Here's a thought. The third week of October is fall break. The girls have a full week off from school. We've been talking about going to Knott's Berry Farm and Disneyland. My vacation request was approved. I'm not sure about Noah, I mean, if he can make it or not."

She pursed her lips. "That's why we haven't made any solid plans yet. Fire season is so unpredictable, especially this year."

Ashley shrugged her shoulders. "It's tough for Emma and Katie. All their friends are planning to do something fun as a family go to an amusement park or camping. It's like we're in limbo, waiting to see if Noah will be available."

"That *is* a quandary. Hmm, how about this?" He grasped Ashley's elbow. "I'm not sure if I mentioned this or not, but I own a six-seat twin-engine airplane. I got my private pilot's license eight years ago. It makes it easier for me to travel for business. I would love to fly up and bring all of you back to LA for the week."

Ashley stared at him. "Wow! That's amazing. That sounds like celebrity kind of stuff." She shook her head. "It would be a lot of fun, but we can't go without Noah. It wouldn't be right. I really doubt he'll be released from the fire. It's all right. The girls and I will find something fun to do around here."

Steve shrugged. "Well, if anything changes, the offer still stands."

Emma and Katie poked their head around the corner.

Emma looked up at her with her big brown eyes. "Mom, please, can we go? Dad is always gone, and we never get to plan anything fun. He won't mind if we go without him."

"Please?" Katie squinted her face tightly. "*Please!* I beg you."

"You're such a little actress." Ashley's mouth twitched, holding in a chuckle.

Steve grinned. "You can all stay at my house if you'd like. There's plenty of room and a pool where the girls could enjoy cooling off. My daughters are like fishes. I can't keep them out of the water."

"Please, Mom?" The girls clasped their hands and pouted their lips. "Please?"

"Girls, you know I can't agree to anything like this without discussing it with your dad." Turning to Steve, she smiled warmly. "We don't want to impose. If it works out for us to come, we'll stay in a hotel."

"Sure, whatever you feel comfortable with. Either way, it would be so much fun for both of our families."

Opening the door, she patted his back. "I'll talk with Noah about it and let you know what he says."

Steve smiled. "Sounds fantastic. Stay in touch, and I'll pencil those dates in. Thanks again." With a quick wave, he turned and bounded down the front steps into the night.

Ashley turned off the lights and headed into her bedroom with a smile on her face. The trip to LA would be so much fun. She would try to talk to Noah about it tomorrow. The girls would love it. An adventure to look forward to.

8

Ashley awoke to Trina anxiously meowing in her face and frantically pawing the covers as if to say "Feed me... Now!" She yawned and threw back the blankets. Entering the kitchen, she discovered not only was the food dish empty, but the water bowl was bone dry as well.

Climbing the stairs, she strode into Katie's room and flung open the curtains. "Good morning, sunshine. It seems like someone forgot to do her chores last night."

Katie quickly thrust her arms under the covers with a secretive guilty expression on her face. "Sorry, Mom. I'll get to it right away."

Ashley simultaneously noticed Katie's odd demeanor in addition to an extra wire cage on the desk in her bedroom.

"What's this?" As she took a closer peek, she realized the cage had a nest of squirming pink rats hidden in the sawdust bottom.

"It's just for a few days."

"You did not have my permission, and you know the rules." Ashley shuddered.

Just as she started to walk out of Katie's bedroom door, a flash of brown fur with a long gray stringy tail dashed across Ashley's bare feet and down the hallway. She let out a loud shriek and jumped backward as Trina streaked by, chasing her prey. Katie followed in a flash, swooping the rat up, narrowly saving it from attack. Nikki and Callie dashed up the stairs, barking wildly, and ready to defend their territory.

Emma walked out of her room into the noisy chaos of barking dogs, rubbing her eyes. "What's going on?"

"Oh, just another routine morning at the zoo." Ashley turned to Katie. "Those rats need to go back to their owner. Today."

Emma let out a screech. "What? I had rats next to my room? Yuck!" She stomped back to her bedroom in disgust.

Katie looked mournfully at her from under the covers. "Okay, Mom. Sorry."

As Ashley's heart rate and blood pressure normalized, she had to chuckle at Katie's love for all creatures.

Later that morning, as Ashley was cleaning up the breakfast dishes, Emma approached her again about taking dance classes after school. "I know you need to discuss this with Dad, but he hasn't been here for over a week, and the classes I want to take start in two days. If I'm going to be able to take them, I really need to sign up today and get the leotard and shoes. Do you think there's any way you can make this decision without him?"

Emma had such sweet sincerity in her dark brown eyes that Ashley couldn't say no.

Grinning at her daughter, she clapped her hands. "Yes, I think we can! Tell you what, I'll pick you up from school today, and we'll go over to the dance studio and sign you up for classes. Then we can go buy what you need to start. How does that sound?"

"Thank you, Mom. I'm so excited! I'm going to call Olivia and Charlotte." Emma gave her a huge hug and dashed up the stairs.

*****

Noah and his crew were still fighting the Lake Fire, as it was now named, without much success at containment. Dry north winds whipped up throughout the day and night with gusts up to eighty miles per hour. Low humidity and high winds had caused extreme fire weather conditions. In an effort to reduce the risk, the power company had mandated rolling outages, leaving everyone in the dark, without electricity to run their appliances or pump gas at the station.

Nursing homes and hospitals evacuated, businesses closed, and grocery stores ran out of supplies. Worst of all, some homes and businesses were being looted. From his vantage point at fire camp, the once pretty lakeside community was now an apocalyptic scene of ash and smoldering ruins, entire neighborhoods consumed within minutes. There had already been dozens of fatalities from those unable or unwilling to evacuate.

A Medivac helicopter lifted away, carrying a firefighter. Noah pressed grimy fingertips over his weary eyes. His team of firefighters had fought against all odds through the night as raining ash stung and burned any unprotected flesh.

Crews had been fighting this fire for over a week now. All were exhausted beyond measure. Many were experienced firefighters, but he was overseeing some new seasonal firefighters, fresh out of high school. The combination of youth, adrenaline, and fatigue was a dangerous cocktail.

Sometime after midnight, Noah had sat on a rocky outcropping, drinking lukewarm water from his canteen, when the night air filled with a horrific scream. He jumped off the rocks and ran toward the sound, fearing the worst. When he arrived at the scene, his nostrils clenched with the smell of smoke and burned flesh.

While patrolling part of the fire line, Drew Young, a first season firefighter, had fallen into a stump hole, the remains of a tree burned so hot and completely it had left a sheen of white ash obscuring a pit of hot coals beneath.

His right leg was buried to the knee. His team members managed to extricate him, but several suffered burns on themselves during the rescue process. The scream faded into weak groans of agony.

Noah dropped to his knees and pressed his second and third finger to Drew's jugular. "His pulse is rapid, and his skin is cool and clammy." He turned to his captain. "Call for medivac ASAP. He's in shock. We need to get him to the hospital."

Taking charge of the scene, he barked out orders.

"Steven, elevate his legs with a backpack to increase blood flow to his vital organs."

"Roger." Steven gingerly lifted the victim's leg while another slid the backpack in place.

"Now cover him with a thermal blanket from your emergency pack."

"Affirmative."

"Matt and John, go back to the fire engine and get the Stokes Litter. We need to get him out of here and down to the camp as soon as we can."

"On our way, Chief." They ran back down the fire line and out into the dark, flashlights cutting bright beams through the smoke.

Noah crouched next to Andrew's side and clutched his hand. "Hang on, son. I know it hurts. Help is on the way. We're arranging for a medivac flight right now."

Drew looked up at Noah, nodded faintly, and then faded into unconsciousness. Returning with the litter, four firefighters expertly hoisted Drew onto it and secured him. Noah led the way as they carefully carried him through the woods back to the waiting pickup for transport to the lighted helipad at fire camp.

As the medivac helicopter lifted off into the night, Noah prayed. "Please, Lord. Keep him alive to get the medical care he needs. Please heal him and the others injured."

Hours later, Noah was attempting to get some sleep when he received a call from the Command Center with an update. "The docs don't think they can save Drew's leg, and it's touch and go whether he'll survive. He's in the burn unit. Firefighters Stone and Green had second and third degree burns on their lower arms. They were also admitted to the Burn Unit. We'll give you updates as they come."

"Copy. Thanks for the update." Noah ended the call and laid back down on the bed.

In addition to exhaustion and severe fire conditions, another thought weighed on his mind. It was unlikely, despite his approved time off, that he and Ashley would be celebrating their anniversary together. In the morning, he'd call her and suggest they postpone their plans. This would cause another rift, but there weren't any other options.

Ironically, Noah had suggested early October as their wedding date because traditionally, fire season had wound down, air attack bases closed, and seasonal firefighters were released by then. Over the past decade, as the climate became warmer, wind events became more frequent. People built their dream homes in remote wooded areas without adequate fire clearance. Fire season grew longer and longer and more dangerous.

Now October was notorious for being the worst month for frequent red flag fire weather. He felt bad as he knew Ashley had spent a lot of time making plans and coordinating care for their daughters for their anniversary getaway.

Noah rubbed his stinging eyes. *God knows I could use a break, and our marriage certainly needs some attention.* Fire season was taking a toll on him and all the other firefighters, all of them missed their families and had to cancel plans.

He appreciated how Ashley juggled their daughters' schedules, her career, and care of the household. She was a strong, independent woman, but the challenges of his job put a strain on their relationship. At the moment, there was absolutely nothing he could do about it.

Although his body ached with fatigue and stress, his mind would not shut off. Drew's screaming agony and the smell of burnt flesh replayed in his head over and over. Thrusting the cover off one of his legs to cool his body, Noah reflected on his childhood and career as a firefighter.

He had been raised in the country with four older brothers. In the morning, after chores were completed, the boys would head down to the river to fish or hike for hours in the mountains. They were a tight-knit family raised by their loving parents Todd and Mary. Todd was mountain man with no fear of the wild. His mother was a homemaker who was known countywide for her apple and berry pies. Every year, she would come home from the county fair with blue ribbons in hand. His dad was a firefighter and his hero. Growing up, he wanted to follow in his footsteps.

His first summer after high-school graduation, Noah applied for a seasonal firefighter position, hoping to earn enough money for his first year of college. After going through the interview process, he was hired. It was long hard days of labor in the hot sun cutting fire line and doing all the grunt work. Being the newbie, Noah got assigned the dirty jobs such as cleaning the bathrooms in the barracks, rolling the fire hoses after an incident, and washing and waxing the fire engines.

Three months later, he had gained five pounds of lean muscle, respect from his fellow firefighters, and a new life perspective. He shed teenage innocence over the course of the summer, growing into a mature young adult. He loved the action of the call alarm going off. Racing to pull up his turn-out gear, he'd jump into his assigned seat on the engine, heart beating fast. Structure fires and wildland fires were his favorite calls. He loved the teamwork and camaraderie of working hard and helping those in need.

Even after earning enough for his first year of college, he returned every summer to work as a seasonal firefighter. Every fall, he would return to college, support himself, and pay for tuition and books. For extra income, he worked on campus driving a bus, and clearing tables at the coffee shop. He determined to set himself up for success and did not want to financially impact his family who were already living on a shoestring with four younger siblings at home.

Two hard years later, he graduated top of his class with an associate degree in fire science and his Emergency Medical Service Credential. His family cheered loudly, holding up signs with loud whoops and whistles as his name was called. Noah applied to the state fire department his last winter of college and was placed on the waiting list of potential candidates for full-time positions.

In the spring, he was contacted for an interview. Sitting on the interview board panel, sweat trickled down his back as they grilled him about his qualifications, work experience, ethics, and how he would tolerate long periods of time on fires. They questioned how he would respond to life in the barracks and his perspective of being a team player.

This was a trophy position he could build his career on. It wasn't easy to break in at the entry level. Hundreds of young hopeful firefighters had applied for the few available positions. Fortunately for Noah, he had built up a reputation of being a solid hardworking individual with a stellar list of accomplishments and references. Selected and offered the position, his career as a firefighter was official.

Finally, falling into an exhausted sleep, Noah's dreams were filled with vivid images—someone screaming, walls of flames dwarfing the heavily wooded forests, and burning flesh. Waking up in a sweat, he found the covers thrown off the bed, his heart pounding in his chest. He glanced at the bedside clock: 4:00 a.m. He had only slept a few hours after receiving the update from the Command Center, and he had to be up again in less than an hour.

After taking several long slugs of water from the bottle on his nightstand, his heart rate lowered. *Just a dream…a bad dream which unfortunately had also been reality.* Laying his head back on the pillow, he shut his eyes and tried to sleep, but the earlier events of the night continued to haunt him.

9

Ashley leaned back in her work chair and stretched her arms. The newly hired neonatologist, Dr. Reed, had turned out to be a real prima donna. Multiple night shift nurses had submitted formal complaints describing her unacceptable and unsafe bully behaviors. Being a NICU nurse was challenging enough. The pompous attitude and undermining behavior of Dr. Reed had created a toxic work environment and needed to be stopped.

Ashley mentally prepared for the meeting scheduled to start in ten minutes. Also attending the meeting with Dr. Reed were the NICU Director, Dr. Cook, and the NICU nursing supervisor. With the amount of hard proof and complaints lodged, it was likely Dr. Reed would be put on probation or possibly suspended. Ashley didn't look forward to the meeting, but she was prepared, as always, to defend her staff and maintain a safe workplace environment. The staff knew she was fair and had their backs.

Ashley tried to relax for a few minutes, her mind drifting to Noah and their upcoming anniversary. They had spoken this morning. Considering the nightly news coverage, she was concerned for Noah. This was quickly becoming one of the worst fire seasons in history.

During their video chat that morning, she had mentioned the LA trip to Noah.

"I don't really like the idea of you two spending time together when I'm not there. It seems to me like he's trying to reconnect with you."

"Oh no, he's just a friend." She laughed. "Don't you trust me? The girls are super-excited."

"It's not that I don't trust you. I don't trust *him*. Flying down in his private plane and spending a whole week hanging out in his fancy house and expensive yacht? It's a little over the top, you know?"

Ashley sighed and tried to keep the bitterness from her tone. "If you feel that strongly, we won't go. We'll find something fun to do here. It's just all the girls' friends have fun family plans, and none of them will be around. But we'll manage, I guess, as usual."

"Ashley, I love you and trust you. It's not fair to you or the girls that I'm always gone and missing out on important times. You should go. I want you and the girls to go…and have a great time."

Ashley clenched the phone. "You sure?"

"Yes, I'm sure."

"Thanks, Noah. The girls would have been so disappointed if we had to cancel."

Noah hung his head, looking utterly exhausted. "Understood. Look, I have to get back. Love you all."

"We love you too. Take care of yourself. You belong to me." She blew him a kiss and ended the call.

*****

Ashley headed into her office a few minutes before the meeting. Sitting at her desk, she rested the heels of her hands against her forehead. Desperately, she missed her husband and couldn't stop worrying about his safety. *He must be utterly exhausted.* She knew that could be a set-up for disaster; the danger was real and extreme.

Ashley rubbed her eyes and took some deep calming breaths. She took a few sips from her water bottle, stood, squared her shoulders, and headed to the conference room.

The meeting turned out to be as difficult as anticipated. Dr. Reed ran through an emotional discourse of arrogance, denial, anger, tears, and thinly veiled threats as the complaints lodged were reviewed. One thing Ashley could not abide was people not taking ownership of their actions. Dr. Reed took no responsibility and showed her true colors. In the end, everyone unanimously agreed it was time to part ways with no letter of recommendation.

As Dr. Reed flounced out of the meeting with terse parting comments, there was a collective sigh.

"Well, back to the recruiting drawing board," Dr. Cook said.

"Better to spend extra time looking for the right fit than putting out all the fires Dr. Reed created." Ashley glanced at the clock and shot to her feet. "Got to dash. Noah's gone, and I'm late picking up the girls." With a wave of her hand, she strode out of the room. "See you all tomorrow."

The door closed. *Shoot! My keys.* Ashley spun around to grab them from the table, but hearing her name mentioned, she paused with her hand on the door handle.

"Wow! She's *always* picking up the pieces. Her husband is gone all the time."

"I thought I had it rough, but at least I know when my shift starts and ends."

Ashley's face flushed. She opened the door, briskly strode over to the table, and grabbed her keys. "Guess I couldn't get too far without these." With another wave, she left.

Ashley pulled up to the school's curbside and noted Emma and Katie were the last students waiting to be picked up. Mrs. Johnson, the supervising yard teacher, peered anxiously at her watch, leaving the moment she spotted Ashley's arrival.

"Hi, girls! Sorry I'm late. Work lasted longer than expected. How was your day?"

Emma crossed her arms over her chest and lifted her chin. "We're always the last ones here lately. It seems like work is more important to you and Dad than we are!"

Ashley's mouth dropped. "Emma! That is uncalled for. Your dad and I are doing our best, and you and Katie both know how much we love you."

Emma continued to pout. "It's embarrassing. All the other kids are long gone, and Mrs. Johnson was wondering if you would even show up. She had meetings and stuff she had to do."

Ashley hated the fact that her kids were the last ones picked up. She promised herself long ago that wouldn't happen.

Irritably, she turned to face the girls. "May I remind you Dad's and my job pay for all the extras you both enjoy such as horseback riding and dance? We both have demanding jobs that require juggling our schedules, but we *always* put you girls first." She pounded her hand on the steering wheel. Ashley became angrier and angrier. "Neither of you have ever had to want for anything." Tears streamed down her cheeks. "My life is entirely devoted to caring for our family!" She grabbed a Kleenex, crossed her arms on the steering wheel, and folded her head on top of her hands.

Emma burst into tears. "I'm sorry. That was a stupid thing to say, and I didn't mean it. It's just Dad is gone *all* the time, and you *always* seem so stressed."

Katie chimed in, "We love you, and you're the best. Please don't cry."

Ashley sniffled for a few more seconds and blew her nose. She drew a few ragged breaths. "It's been a long day for everyone."

Still stinging from Emma's sharp comments, she put the car into drive and threaded her way through the school parking lot. Her hands tightened on the steering wheel. "Let's go home and regroup. We're all hungry and tired."

*****

Later that evening, after dinner was prepared, cleaned up, pets fed, homework finished, lunches packed, laundry folded, baths and showers completed, tomorrow's clothes set out, and girls tucked into bed, Ashley wearily curled up in her favorite chair with a mug of Sleepy Time tea. As she scanned her e-mails, a message from Steve popped up.

Hey, Ash,

Thank you again for a fantastic meal and company the other night. Great to see you and your family. I've been following the Lake Fire, and it looks devastating. Is Noah still out there? Praying for everyone affected and for safety for all the firefighters.

Are you still considering coming to LA? Not sure if you had a chance to speak to Noah. If you decide to come, I could fly up on Monday to pick you up. I looked at my schedule and rearranged a few things. The invitation to stay at my house is still open. There's plenty of room and a pool the girls would love. The dogs are more than welcome to come too. I have a housekeeper who can watch them when we're gone. We can go to the amusement parks, go sailing on my boat, fly out to Catalina Island for a day, or do whatever you'd like. Looking forward to hearing from you soon.

Warm regards,
Steve

Rearranged his schedule? The words jumped out at Ashley. She hadn't heard that from Noah for years. Instead, Ashley always rearranged *her* schedule to accommodate his. *That's a refreshing change. Steve has a busy schedule and demanding job as well. That speaks volumes about him.* She smiled and typed up a quick reply.

Hey Steve,

That sounds wonderful! Are you sure about the dogs? If so, that's great. Noah is still on the fire with no containment, so hard to say if he'll be back by then or not, but he gave us his blessing to come out. We still think it would be best if the girls and I stayed at a hotel, so I'll do some checking around for availability. Thank you! We'll talk soon.

Ashley

Suddenly the future looked much brighter. *Finally, something fun planned that we can count on.*

10

On the fire, no day or night existed. The smoky and gray atmosphere was only illuminated by glowing cinders and swirls of choking hot ash. The sun vanished behind the murky air, making the surroundings look like a war zone.

Officially, the Lake Fire was now the worst wildland fire in United States history. Over a hundred fatalities and thousands of homes and businesses had been lost.

After a forty-eight-hour shift of backbreaking labor, Noah and his crew trudged into camp for a hot meal, a cool shower, and some rest. Standing in the chow line, Noah turned to a fellow teammate. "Hey, Greg, did you hear President Thomas and his entourage are coming tomorrow?"

"Yeah, that's going to add a lot of logistics."

Noah nodded as he piled his plate high with steak, potatoes, beans, salad, and bread. "I'm starving, dude." He snagged two pieces of pie before sitting down to shovel the food into his depleted body.

"Me too." Greg lifted his dinner roll as if to toast him.

Minutes went by as both men focused on eating. After he ate the last forkful of pie, Noah wiped his mouth and patted his stomach.

"Better," he said with a burp. "Did you hear the weather briefing for tomorrow? Single digit humidity levels, highs in the low hundreds, and wind gusts up to sixty miles per hour! I honestly think this is the worst fire I've ever been on, and that says a lot."

"Agreed." Greg piled his napkins and silverware on his plate and stood. "Well, I'm going to bed. Tomorrow is going to be another snarly day to attack it again."

After his stomach was full, the prospect of showering before passing out in bed seemed too exhausting until he caught a whiff of himself. *Not an option.* He settled in to wait his turn in the long line for the portable showers.

"Okay, Chief, you're up." The attendant monitoring the showers finally waved him into an open cubicle.

As the water swept away two days' worth of soot and grime, a wave of homesickness washed over him as well. After showering, Noah felt slightly more grounded. He didn't even remember lying down on his bed and falling fast asleep.

*****

At seven the following day, Noah listened intently to the Planning Section Chief's daily operations briefing. The news wasn't good. Overnight, the fire had raged on with more lives and property lost. Additionally, tragedy had struck.

"It's with a heavy heart and condolences to the Acer family that I have to inform you all that Mike Acer suffered a fatal injury last night."

Audible gasps filled the room as the chief continued. "Many of you worked side by side with Mike, a top-notch heavy fire equipment operator. He had been cutting line in poor visibility in steep terrain. Unfortunately, his bulldozer tracks had slipped sideways on a slick slate rock outcropping, slid downhill, hit a boulder, and flipped."

Noah hung his head. "No, not Mike." His heart ached thinking of Mike's widow and family of three young children growing up without their dad.

A fellow firefighter clasped Noah's shoulder, "I know, man. He was one of the good ones…the best."

Noah closed his eyes. *Dear Lord, please be with Mike's family. Comfort them through this tragic loss.* Brushing the tears from his eyes with his knuckles, he straightened in his chair, trying to focus on the remainder of the briefing.

The Planning Section Chief continued, "Air Force One is scheduled to fly over the incident around 10:45 this morning with the President arriving at Incident Base by 1300 hours." In a stern voice, he continued, "I shouldn't have to tell you this means no aircraft support over the incident between 1030 and 1100 hours at least because of the temporary flight restriction always in place around Air Force One. Plan accordingly."

Noah glanced around the room at the other division supervisors not masking the visible frustration on their faces. *Great! That's right when we are going to need the aircraft support.*

"I know this is going to be a huge distraction and media circus. But the commander-in-chief wants to see firsthand the effects of the fire to show support for all the fire personnel."

Noah and others in the room nodded.

"The weather will not be in our favor as the afternoon progresses. Expect more red flag conditions with prevailing winds from the north. We just have to keep fighting for containment."

Noah reviewed his plan of attack for his crews. This was going to be a long all-out battle. While he sat in the briefing, his mind drifted as other logistical details that didn't involve him or his crew were discussed.

He recalled that in his last two decades of firefighting, he had only asked to be released once for Katie's birth. Ashley's pregnancy had been complicated, and the delivery was high risk. Two weeks before Katie's due date, Noah was ordered to a fire in a very remote area with steep canyons. The crews were helicoptered in and off the fire in forty-eight-hour shifts. Both Noah and Ashley became more anxious as Katie's due date approached and the fire continued to rage. Noah went to his supervisor and requested to be released from the fire.

Fortunately, his crusty supervisor had known Noah since he was a young seasonal firefighter. He had observed his work ethic and dedication to his career and pulled the necessary strings, releasing Noah just in time to get home and support Ashley with the birth.

The sense of helplessness he felt as Katie's heart rate started dropping was still fresh in his memory. The decision was immediately made to deliver via an emergency C-section. It was terrifying. He was concerned he would lose the woman he loved *and* their child.

He never left her side—praying, squeezing her hand, and whispering words of comfort and support.

Katie was born with bluish lips, feet, and hands. The umbilical cord had been looped around her neck twice, obstructing the blood flow. Katie was resuscitated and intubated while Ashley and Noah watched helplessly. Once stabilized, the transport team whisked her to the NICU.

They were so relieved when Katie showed signs of recovery. It wrenched Noah's heart to see their baby lying on the warming table in the NICU instead of in Ashley's arms. He stayed by Ashley's side, sleeping in a chair next to her bed, alert to her every need while she was still in the hospital. She had been a warrior. It was the least he could do.

Noah's parents had come to take care of Emma so Noah and Ashley could fully focus on Katie. His parents were wonderful and took care of everything at home. Emma was so excited the day Katie had been taken out of the Isolette, bundled in blankets, and placed in her arms. She held her while her dad sat next to her with a watchful eye. In wonder, she stroked her sister's soft cheek and kissed her.

Long hours were spent in the NICU bonding with Katie and, thankfully, seeing her get stronger every day. Dressing Katie in her pink coming-home outfit, Emma was beside herself in her new role as big sister.

She brushed Katie's downy blond hair and marveled at her tiny nail beds. "This is my little sister," she joyfully announced to every-one who entered the room as Ashley's NICU coworkers and friends gathered to send the family home with congratulations and good wishes.

"Thank you all so much for everything." Ashley smiled, waving goodbye as she was wheeled out of the hospital with Katie in her lap.

"You have all been so wonderful. Thank you, from the bot-tom of my heart." Noah had rapped his fist over his heart and raced downstairs to bring the car around. Buckled in, he glanced in the rearview mirror at his newborn daughter, smiled at Ashley, and put the car into drive.

Noah stirred as sounds of the metal chairs shifted, and people stood and left to return to their duties. He longed for those innocent days.

*****

Since he had been promoted two years ago to Battalion Chief, Noah's job on large fires was usually as a division supervisor, which entailed managing the fire engines, fire crews, and other equipment assigned to his division.

As he waited for his crew to assemble, he pulled out his cell to call Ashley. She answered on the second ring.

"Hi, babe! I was hoping I could reach you before my next shift started. It's been crazy here. I miss you and the girls so much. How are you?"

"We're doing fine." Her familiar lyrical voice soothed him like nothing else could. "Miss you like crazy. The news we're seeing about the fire is scary. Are you all right?"

"Yeah, it's going to be a long haul, but I slept well last night. More like I actually went into a coma for ten hours!" He laughed and then swallowed hard. "Ashley, I have some bad news."

She let out a shaky breath. "What is it?"

Steeling himself, he broke the news. "Mike Acer had an accident last night cutting line. The bulldozer slipped on some rocks, flipped, and he was killed."

There was a long pause, then Ashley choked out, "Oh, Noah, I'm so sorry. Mike was a wonderful man. This is tragic! Are you doing all right?"

"Just like you, I'm sad. Such a great guy. He was a believer, so he's with the Lord…but his wife…and children—" His voice trailed off.

"I'll stop by their house with some food. His daughter Sammy is in Katie's class. Maybe I can help with school pick up or drop off. Oh my. This is so sad."

Tears again blurred Noah's eyes as he thought of his friend and how his death would affect his wife and family. Wiping away the tears, he slumped against his chair. *Too many lives over the years lost way too early.*

Ashley broke the silence he'd let stretch between them. "Honey, I wish I could be with you. I'm sending you my love. Be safe, please."

"I'll do my best. This fire is the worst I've seen." Noah released a heavy sigh. "But we will win this war. Eventually."

Ashley had gone quiet again. "Noah, I hate to bring this up now after such bad news, but it's so hard for us to connect. I wish you were here, right by my side, so I could give you a huge hug and kiss. I miss you so much, and I'm worried about you. Really worried."

Noah raked his fingers through his hair. "I miss you like crazy too. I'd kill for that hug." With a tired sigh, he longed for home. "Go ahead, babe. What is it?"

She cleared her throat. "It's about the trip to LA. The last time we spoke about it, you had said you couldn't go, but you knew how excited the girls were about the trip."

"Yes." Noah's jaw tightened. "I did."

"I e-mailed Steve to say we can come, but when I started searching for a hotel in the area, everything is booked solid. It looks like everyone else had the same plan to go to Disneyland during fall break." She took a deep breath. "Steve offered for us to stay at his house. Apparently, he has a huge home with plenty of room and a pool which you know the girls would love." Rushing her words, she pressed on, "I totally understand if you don't feel comfortable with that. Just say the word, and we won't go."

Noah stared at the smoke filling the horizon.

"Noah? Are you still there?"

He cleared his throat and pondered his response. Was he okay with his wife's former boyfriend flying his family in his fancy private plane, taking them sailing on his yacht, and having them stay at his house for a week while Noah was in the firefight of his life? Jealousy reared its ugly head. *No, I am* not *okay with that. That's* my *family.*

"Noah, can you hear me?"

"Sorry, babe. I got distracted. It's a war zone around here." Sucking in his pride and jealous anger, Noah chose his words carefully. "Of course I want you and the girls to go. That sounds fantastic. At the rate things are going, I highly doubt that we'll be released, so please go ahead with your plans. You all deserve some fun, and I trust you."

"Well, it certainly won't be as fun without you. I wish you could go. And, of course, you should trust me. Steve is just an old friend. Emma and Katie are so excited and eager to meet his daughters. Did I mention Nikki and Callie are coming too? We'll be quite the motley group." Ashley laughed.

His crew members were gathering, so he needed to end the call. "You know how much I love you and the girls. I wish I was with you. Please hug and kiss them for me. I'll call you again when I can. Bye." He hung up the phone, took a deep breath, and turned to his crew. "Okay, let's go fight fire! We gotta get this thing out so we can all go home!"

His crew sent up a rallying cry, "Yeah! Let's do this!"

Off they went for another brutal forty-eight-hour shift of fighting the widow-maker.

11

Ashley peered at her work computer screen, trying to catch up on e-mails. A knock on the door announced the arrival of her friend Laurie. "Hey, girlfriend. Do you have a few minutes for a coffee break and chat?"

Ashley swiveled in her chair and smiled. "Yes. Please save me from slow death by e-mail. I'm smothering in all this minutia."

She walked over to the sink and filled her electric teapot with water. "What would you like?" She held out her basket of assorted teas and coffees to Laurie.

Laurie selected a medium blend brew. Minutes later, Ashley poured the steaming water into mugs, dropping an Earl Grey teabag into hers and an instant coffee bag into Laurie's. She showed Laurie where she kept the sugar and creamer.

Laurie shook her head. "Black is fine. Thanks."

They sat in adjacent chairs and put their feet up on hassocks, enjoying the short respite from their busy day. A few minutes of chit-chat later, Laurie zeroed in on what she wanted to talk about.

"So how does Noah *really* feel about your trip to LA with Steve? My David would be unhappy," she said with full emphasis on the word *unhappy.*

Laurie crossed her legs and swiped her phone for messages. Finding none, she glanced up at Ashley. "After all, you and Steve were almost engaged at one point. This whole fly you down in his private plane, sail on his yacht, and stay in his mansion in LA plan sounds pretty sexy." Laurie gave her a questioning look. "Are you *sure* about this, Ashley?"

Ashley swiveled her head, facing her friend directly. "Oh, come on, Laurie! You're making far more out of this than a simple invitation from a family friend. Yes, it's going to be a super-sexy trip with me and the girls and our two dogs. Don't forget, Steve's two kids are going to be there as well!" she said sarcastically. "It's going to be more like a zoo than anything."

Laurie continued her rant. "So are you the stand-in stepmom of the crowd or what?"

Ashley began to simmer. "Laurie, you are way out of line! You know my heart and my relationship with Noah. I'll admit it can be rough with him being gone for long periods with practically no notice, but I would never cheat on him!" She set her cup down hard, tea sloshing over the edge. "We trust each other, and he is perfectly okay with the girls and me going to LA. I'm not going to allow you or anyone else to guilt-trip me!"

Laurie gave her a doubtful look. "I would just *hate* to see this visit affect your and Noah's relationship. I'm sharing with you that if either David or I went on a trip like this with an old flame, even if it was innocent, it would *hurt* our marriage...our *trust*." Swinging her feet off the hassock, Laurie leaned forward and took Ashley's hand. Her eyes emoted sincerity. "It's tough carrying the burden of work and family. Believe me, I get it. But fire season will end, and you and Noah will have time to work on your marriage." She held up a finger as Ashley tried to interject. "As a friend, I have one more thing to say. It feels like *cheating*, even if you say it's all innocent. I know how much you love Noah, but it doesn't seem right for you to spend time with Steve without Noah there."

An angry flush rose on Ashley's cheeks.

Laurie crossed her arms tightly, lips pursed. "There. I knew you wouldn't like it, but it's the truth. I think you're making a horrible mistake, Ashley...one you may *regret*."

Sitting back in her chair, Ashley glared at Laurie, then softened. "I appreciate your heart and your concerns. I do. I've thought about this a lot and spoken with Noah. It's just going to be a casual fun time with an old friend and his daughters. Nothing more."

Laurie shook her head with a defeated expression. "Okay. You're a grown woman and responsible for your own choices. Just think about all the angles and how it may appear to other people."

Ashley bristled. "Well, I think 'other people' should mind their own business and clean up their own backyards. That's what I think." Steam practically blew out of her ears. "It's easy to make judgments until you're in someone else's shoes!"

Laurie shrugged her shoulders and picked at her cuticles. "Just saying. Think about how this looks. I've seen Steve a few times when he's been here working and teaching. It's hard to miss him. He is *sooo* good-looking." Laurie's eyebrows raised. "And you know the hospital can be a rumor mill. But *most* of all, I care about you, Noah, and your family."

The overhead speaker suddenly announced, "Code Blue NICU. Code Blue NICU."

Laurie and Ashley rushed down the hall. Liz, the RN day shift coordinator met them as they swept through the key lock entry and threw on their cover gowns. As they scrubbed into the unit, she gave them a quick report. "Bed B-4 is coding again. Female, twenty-four-week micro-preemie transported last night. Baby Wilson has been unstable since arrival. We suspect sepsis and are awaiting twenty-four-hour blood cultures. Maternal membranes ruptured thirty-six hours before delivery, and blood pressure has been unstable. Baby Wilson is on a dopamine drip, but her blood pressure keeps falling, and carbon dioxide levels rising. Fresh frozen plasma has been ordered STAT, and the code Team is hand ventilating."

Ashley nodded. "Please notify Dr. Cook."

Ashley turned to the Code Blue infusion RN, Stacy. "Please administer epinephrine and sodium bicarbonate per body weight protocol slow IV push and recheck the arterial blood gas."

Stacy hurriedly nodded and repeated the directions while drawing up the medications.

Ashley continued to direct the team. "Please repeat the meds every five minutes."

"Repeating meds every five minutes." Stacy nodded at the scribe RN who was tracking the code and recording the Code Blue team efforts and medications administered.

Ashley scrutinized the monitors, noting the infant's blood pressure was too low. "Increase the dopamine drip infusion to maintain mean blood pressure at thirty millimeters of mercury."

"Dopamine drip increased. Monitoring mean blood pressure," Stacy briskly informed the team.

"Hmm," Ashley watched the monitors intently. "Blood pressure is still borderline. Administer ten milliliters of fresh frozen plasma to be administered slow IV push STAT upon its arrival from pharmacy."

Stacy repeated, "Ten milliliters fresh frozen plasma ordered to be administered slow IV push STAT upon arrival."

Ashley turned to the respiratory therapist. "Okay, your ventilations are effective, but I think we need to increase the rate. CO_2 levels are elevated."

The RN working as the official code scribe and runner for lab work and medications returned from the pharmacy with the plasma.

Stacy called out, "Ten milliliters fresh frozen plasma being administered slow IV push. Blood pressure is still dropping. Dopamine drip is titrated to the highest level."

Ashley gestured at Liz, the charge nurse, to come closer. "I'm thinking this is overwhelming sepsis. Please call the lab and ask them for a quick response ID of the blood culture STAT."

Liz nodded and rushed off to make the call.

Ashley encouraged the team. "Everyone is doing a wonderful job. Keep up the effort. We're trying to get more information about Baby Wilson's lab status, so continue the code until you hear otherwise."

The Code Blue Team nodded and continued running the code as a practiced seamless operation. Dr. Cook arrived at scene and was briefed by Ashley and Liz. The runner brought the preliminary blood culture report. As the results were scanned, the team looked at each other in dismay.

"Not good." Dr. Cook shook his head.

Ashley and Liz reluctantly agreed.

Ashley summarized the findings. "Baby Wilson's white blood count is way too high for her to fight on her own. She has already received three doses of strong IV broad spectrum antibiotics and isn't responding. What are your thoughts, Dr. Cook?"

"I think we all realize this is a losing battle," he said. "As I recall, Mrs. Wilson had complications herself and is still hospitalized. I'll make the necessary calls."

He faced the Code Blue Team. "You've all done a fantastic job, but unfortunately, the infection has overwhelmed her ability to fight it. At this point, we need to call the code and let nature take its course." Sadly, he went to his office for the difficult task of informing the family.

Ashley turned to Charlotte, the RN assigned to the baby, who was wiping tears from her eyes. It was never easy. And it was even harder when you were the nurse spending twelve-hour shifts providing intensive nursing. It was impossible not to become attached and feel responsible when a patient was lost. Ashley walked around the warming table to the grieving nurse.

She squeezed Charlotte's shoulder. "You did your best. There was nothing anyone could've done. The prolonged rupture of membranes and extreme prematurity was too overwhelming." Ashley gave her a hug. "Please go take your break. I'll spell you."

Charlotte looked at Ashley with tears streaming down her cheeks. "Thank you, Ashley. I appreciate it."

Dr. Cook returned to the bedside and placed a hand lightly on Ashley's shoulder.

"I just spoke with Baby Wilson's parents. Mom is still hospitalized in critical condition. Dad is at her bedside and doesn't want to leave her. All their immediate family live hours away and couldn't make it here in time." Pursing his lips, Dr. Cook continued. "It is unfortunate, but they understand their daughter will not survive and agree that it is in her best interest to take her off life support. They have requested to FaceTime once she has been taken off support."

Ashley glanced up. "Do the parents know their daughter will be held and comforted the entire time?"

He nodded. "Yes. I told them we have excellent nurses who will treat their daughter as if she was her own."

"Yes, we will. Absolutely. She will be loved all the way to heaven." Her eyes welled with moisture. It never got any easier.

Patting her back again, Dr. Cook blinked back tears. "Thank you."

"All right. Do you want me to disconnect her?"

"Yes. I'll go write the order and transcribe the summary. Thank you."

Ashley nodded and turned to the baby lying on the warming table. "Okay, darling. Let's get you wrapped up and snuggle." Ashley detached the wires and removed the endotracheal tube. She swaddled the baby in a warm blanket and held her in a nearby rocking chair as her last heartbeats faded.

Gently humming a soothing tune, Ashley prayed for the little life taken way too soon. She prayed for comfort and peace for the baby's family. A long time ago, as a young NICU nurse, Ashley had done some intense soul-searching about life and death, questioning why innocent babies and their families suffered. There were no easy answers or earth-shattering revelations. She only knew she was put on this planet to be a nurse and help others, and she would do the best job she could.

When Charlotte came back from her break, she looked somewhat less weary. "Thanks, Ashley. I'm ready to get back to work."

"Anytime," Ashley said. "What a beautiful baby. Let me know if you need anything else, now or later. I'll check back with you."

She quietly left and made the rounds of debriefing with the other Code Blue Team members. A monthly morbidity and mortality meeting would be held later to review findings and evaluate each situation. However, initial debriefing was important, especially for new team members, to work through a tragic loss.

When the extended family arrived, they were moved into a special area of the NICU designed to allow for privacy. Charlotte's other patients were reassigned so she could solely focus on supporting the family and completing necessary documentation. Photographs were taken, footprints and handprints made, and a few locks of hair snipped to create treasured keepsakes. Mom and Dad were on FaceTime from her hospital bed, the hospital chaplain sitting nearby for support.

"Her name is Grace," Mom spoke gently, holding her husband's hand. "Grace Elizabeth Wilson."

"That's a beautiful name," Charlotte whispered.

"Please hold her up to the screen so I can give her one last kiss."

"Absolutely." Charlotte lifted her up as Mom and Dad gave her one last tender kiss.

"We love you, Grace Elizabeth, and always will. May God hold you in the palm of His hand until we see you again.

12

The long workweek and trip preparation behind, Ashley turned toward the girls. "All right. I think we're set. Let's get the dogs and bags in the car and take off for the airport."

Beside themselves, the girls rushed off to grab their suitcases. Ashley took one last glance in the mirror, noting her jeans and T-shirt were fitting better. The smoothies and salads were worth it to lose those stubborn pounds. And the brisk walks around the hospital on her lunch and coffee breaks gave her more energy and helped with toning her muscles. She was feeling and looking better than she had for a long time. The prospect of the long-awaited vacation brought a bright smile to her face.

Steve's sleek airplane touched down gracefully and taxied across the runway. Moments later, he bounded down the steps, greeting the girls with a friendly hug and a kiss on Ashley's cheek.

He laughed as the dogs barked and jumped up his legs, seeking their own attention. "Okay, okay. Your turn." He ruffled their ears and dug into his pocket for a dog treat.

Strong feathered tails thumped fiercely on the tarmac as they wolfed down their treats and eagerly waited for another.

"That's it for now." Steve smiled down at them. "There are more treats waiting for you at the end of the ride." He turned back to Ashley and the girls. "I've been looking forward to this week. Cara and Lexi are so excited and busy planning every moment. If you're ready, let's get onboard and get this party started!"

Ashley slung her bag over her shoulder. "Yes! We're *so* ready."

As the girls and dogs clambered aboard with their suitcases, Ashley gave Steve a hug. "Thank you so much. This is a long-needed respite from our crazy schedules."

He gave her an appreciatory gaze. A soft blush heated her cheeks. It had been a long time since anyone, including Noah, made her feel that way.

*****

What a glorious week. The weather had been perfect. Ashley and Steve's girls swiftly became best friends. The days melted into wonderful memories of sailing, swimming, sunshine, amusement parks, and wonderful family time.

Steve finished the last of the dinner dishes and hung up the dishtowel. He raised his eyebrows at Ashley with a smile. "Want to watch the sunset?"

"Twist my arm!" Ashley giggled. She felt wonderfully carefree and almost giddy.

This past week was more fun than she'd had for—well, a very long time. Steve was a wonderful host. He was so giving, thoughtful, and kind. He treated her like a princess.

Wait a minute! Where did that come from?

Ashley shook her head in an effort to clear her thoughts. They had spent the day at the amusement park. Over dinner, the girls had teased her mercilessly for her girlish screams on the roller coaster.

"Mom! I've never seen you be afraid of anything!" Katie mimicked her mom's screams.

Ashley was laughing so hard tears streaming down her cheeks. As the girls raced outside for one last swim in the pool, Steve leaned over and wiped the tears of laughter from her eyes with his index finger.

He whispered, "I love seeing you so happy."

Ashley had changed the subject by grabbing her water bottle and taking a swig. But now, as they walked out to the patio, wine glasses in hand, it was becoming all too clear.

"Steve, I think we need to talk."

"Sure," he replied, guiding her to a comfortable lounge chair and setting the bottle of wine between them. The air was full of happy squeals of laughter as the dogs jumped in the pool, chasing balls. "I've been wanting to talk to you as well. May I go first?"

She nodded, suddenly uncomfortable with the way he was looking at her. She swallowed and focused her attention on her cuticles, pushing her nail down on the half-moons.

"Ashley, this past week with you and the girls has honestly been one of the best weeks of my life. Stephanie and I shared some good years, but frankly, I was too consumed with my work, and we just grew apart."

Ashley twisted her wedding ring nervously.

Steve threw his long legs to the side of the lounge chair and leaned forward, lightly clasping Ashley's hands. "I love the way our kids blend together into one happy family. It makes my heart full seeing everyone get along so well and enjoy each other's company." His bright blue eyes sought hers. "In my mind's eye, I can see us as a family, and a lot of that is who you are, Ashley. I see the way you raise your daughters with so much love but yet firm boundaries. You're an intelligent, beautiful, generous woman. I could kick myself for letting you go so many years ago."

Ashley took a sip of water and put up a hand with her palm facing Steve. "Wait, wait."

Steve shook his head, intent on his mission. "I know you love Noah, but I also know you haven't been happy for quite a while. And I find myself wondering if there's any way you would consider breaking it off with him?"

Her mouth opened wide with astonishment. *What is going on?* Stunned, Ashley nearly dropped her water bottle. She set it down shakily on the side table and took a couple of deep breaths to gather her thoughts before responding.

Yes, the past week had been absolutely fabulous, and they had acted like one big family. The girls were happier than she had ever seen and got along so well with Steve's daughters. Of course, it was easy to be happy and have fun when you had a private jet, a fifty-foot luxurious yacht, and a gorgeous oceanfront property.

"Steve, I'm not sure what to say. I certainly never meant to lead you on. You're a wonderful, terrific person and human being, but I love Noah." Standing up, she brushed the front of her shorts. "I'm afraid I made a terrible mistake coming here. I'm sorry."

Steve stood up next to her, lightly placing his palm on her back. "Don't be sorry, Ash, things happen. Just give it some thought. I won't press you, but I had to let you know how I feel."

Ashley quickly stepped away as Katie called out, "Mom! Look at me!" She spiked the volleyball over the pool net, scoring a point.

"Yeah, Katie!" Clapping, she forced a smile, her heart heavy with guilt.

Noah dropped his keys on the side table as he came in the door. "I'm home!"

Shrugging out of his filthy jacket, he threw it on the floor. One by one, he wearily tugged off his equally dirty boots and socks. *These should go straight to the trash.* He grabbed a black garbage bag, carrying it with him to stuff his turnout, uniform, socks, and shoes into the laundry before getting in the shower. Calling out greetings again, he was met with silence. Katrina, their cat, came running and swished her tail against his legs. She took a delicate whiff and jumped back, pink nose twitching.

Noah laughed out loud. "Trina, I can't blame you! I can't even stand myself."

It was 5:00 as he climbed into the shower, the time everyone was usually getting home, chores were being done, and dinner was deliciously bubbling on the stove. There was no note on the chalkboard, and mail was neatly piled on the kitchen counter. *Where is everyone?* The steam built around him as he remembered. "Oh, that's right. Ashley and the girls are in Southern California…with Steve."

A green-eyed grimace crossed his face as he shampooed and scrubbed the weeks of smoke and grit away. *Stop that. They're entitled to have fun and not sit around waiting for you to come home.* He stepped out of the shower and grabbed his towel. Its gray fibers turned black as he dried his body. *Round two.* Turning the shower back on, he headed back in for a second scrubbing.

*****

64

Ashley fretted the entire flight back home. Her thoughts tumbled around like a whirlpool. Part of her was flattered by Steve's proposal. *If married life with Steve was anything like last week, it would be bliss.* Another part blamed herself, admitting perhaps she had opened that door by unconsciously flirting with him, leading him to think she was interested and available.

She felt horribly guilt-ridden. She had basically cheated on Noah while he was risking his life fighting fire and earning an income for their family. How could she throw away all their years together and tear their family apart? Was she actually *thinking* about it? She never should have agreed to go on this vacation. Laurie had tried to warn her. She should have listened. What an awful, selfish person she was. Her stomach twisted in knots.

Steve shut down the aircraft's engine, opened the door, and lowered the staircase. As the girls and dogs scrambled down the steps, he sat down next to Ashley and took her hand in his. "I know you well enough to see you're putting yourself through the wringer. Please don't. You're not at fault. You are who you are, and that's why I fell in love with you all over again. But if you decide to stay with Noah, I'll respect that."

Leaning forward, he touched his forehead to hers. "Meanwhile, I'll be hoping we can share this lifetime together. The ball is in your court, Ash."

Ashley nodded, tears clouding her vision. "Okay," she said with a shaky voice. "Thank you again for everything. It truly was a wonderful week. We appreciate all you did."

"It was my pleasure." He gazed intently into her eyes.

"Come on, Mom! Let's go! The dogs are getting restless."

"Coming!" Ashley looked back at Steve, giving him a weak smile.

"I'll be in touch once I have some time to process everything. Have a safe trip back. Bye." She climbed down the steps and turned toward the girls. "Let's go home."

On the car ride, the girls were too busy texting their friends and chatting about the trip to notice their mother's inner turmoil. When they pulled into the driveway, Noah's fire vehicle was parked in the garage.

"Dad's home!" the girls shouted in unison as they jumped out of the car with the dogs and raced into the house.

Ashley sat in the car for several moments. Plastering on a fake smile, she steeled herself and headed for the front door.

Noah had picked up both of the girls in his strong arms and twirled them around with a huge grin on his face. "I missed you so much! Did you have a good time?"

When Ashley walked in the door, he set the girls down and enveloped her in a hug, kissing her soundly on the lips. "Babe. It's so fantastic to see you! I'm so happy we're all home together. I missed my girls so much."

Nikki and Callie joined the reunion by racing around the huddled group. Noah turned to the dogs and rubbed both of their ears while they barked and jumped, hugging Noah with their front paws.

"Wow! What a homecoming! You all look so tan. I want to hear all about your week."

As Emma and Katie filled him in on the vacation details, Ashley took her luggage to the bedroom, sat on the bed, and pressed her palms to her forehead.

"Please, God," she prayed. "Forgive me. Help me. I'm so confused."

*****

Later that evening, Noah turned to Ashley in bed and put his arms around her, kissing her amorously. "I missed you so much. It's been too long."

Ashley shifted away from him, ending the kiss. "I'm sorry, but I'm not feeling well. I need to sleep."

"I'm sorry, babe. I'm just happy to be here next to you." He gave her one last hug and kissed her on the forehead. "Goodnight, my angel. Sweet dreams."

Noah's snores filled the night air almost immediately.

Ashley rolled on her side, staring into the dark with tears running hotly down her cheeks. *What am I going to do?* The night passed restlessly as she tormented herself with the *what ifs*.

Minutes turned into hours, which turned into days and then weeks. Ashley was anguished by the decision facing her. One day, she was rock-solid that staying with Noah and keeping their family intact was the only logical choice. The next day brought doubts and uncertainty that playing it safe was the right choice. Was she potentially missing out on sharing the rest of her life with her true love?

Hold on a minute! You used to believe Noah was the love of your life. Ashley questioned the voice in her head. *Why did you say "used to?" Is that no longer how you feel?* Back and forth and back and forth, her emotions dizzily swirled around.

Weight melted off her body as even the idea of food nauseated her twisted spent nerves. Worry lines deepened on her forehead. Nighttime was the worst when Steve would enter her dreams, and they would be sailing on his yacht or flying to some exotic destination in his jet or sitting companionably on the back porch, listening to the waves crash on the sand. He was so kind and such a good listener—everything a woman could hope for in a perfect package.

In the morning, she would wake with a smile on her face, remembering her dream. It was a blissful fantasy, not fraught with all the responsibilities and anxieties of her current day-to-day life.

Every night, Noah would try to initiate lovemaking. Ashley would brush him off with vague excuses. "I'm exhausted and need to sleep" or "I have a headache" or "It's that time of the month," or honestly, "I'm not in the mood." She knew he was puzzled by her behavior and sent her secretive curious looks as if trying to figure out her moods.

This morning, while she was making breakfast, he came into the kitchen and wrapped his arms around her from behind, kissing her neck. "Hey, we need to reschedule our anniversary getaway."

"Well, the holidays are coming up soon, and I've been so busy at work." She shrugged. "I honestly don't know when I could get time off."

Holding her tighter, he whispered in her ear, "We need to make time for us…to be us."

Stepping away from him, she flipped the pancakes. "I just can't make any plans now. I need to get to work."

"What's happening, Ash?"

"Nothing. I'm late and need to get going." She handed him the plate of pancakes. "Please make sure the girls get fed before you drive them to school. You'll have to leave in fifteen minutes." She slung her bag over her shoulder and walked out the door. A heavy weight of responsibility mixed with confusion washed over her as she drove to work.

13

Following a long day of meetings and arranging staffing schedules, Ashley dragged through the front door. Setting down her purse and briefcase, she found Noah sitting on the couch, reading a magazine.

"If you have a few minutes, I want to talk with you about our schedules."

He looked up at her and patted the seat next to him. "What's up, babe?"

She sat down, angling her knees toward him. "I've been asked to organize and teach a three-day course on neonatal resuscitation. It's a pretty big deal, actually. There were only thirty slots open to nurses all over California."

"Congratulations! That sounds awesome."

She looked directly in his eyes. "People plan their schedules around this course because it's a requirement if they want to work in labor and delivery. I need to be totally clear of any responsibilities outside of work for those three days because the class starts at 7:00 a.m. and can run late if additional practice time and testing is needed."

He nodded. "I get it. This is important to you and the people in the class. What do you need from me?"

She brushed a lock of wispy hair from her face and squinted. "The class is tentatively scheduled for two weeks from now on Wednesday, November sixteenth, through Friday, November eighteenth. I checked your calendar, and you *should* be on your scheduled days off." She raised her brows. "What do you think? Can I count on you to take the girls to school and pick them up?" She held up her fingers and ticked each item off her list. "They both have after-school activities they'll need to be taken to. Katie has a riding lesson at 4:00 on Wednesday and Friday, and Emma has dance practice for the winter performance every day after school. Are you available?"

Ashley looked at him intently. "Think hard about it. I need to know I can count on you 100 percent. I'll be busy with this class, and I honestly don't know what I'd do if you were unable to last minute. If you can't, tell me now so I can see if Laurie or one of my other friends can help."

He smiled and squeezed her shoulders. "You can count on me, babe. I'll take care of the girls and have a nice hot dinner waiting for you when you come home, followed by a long soak in the tub." He rubbed his hands together in anticipation. "Let's see. I can make my world-famous hamburgers and sweet potato fries or homemade pizza. Which would you prefer?"

"They both sound great. So I have *your promise* that this will be your priority?" Ashley took a deep breath and blew it out slowly. "This is very important to me and my career. My supervisor has been dropping a few comments that I'm not pulling my weight with transports, but your fire season schedule has been so erratic that it's been hard to put myself on the schedule."

"Well, you can tell your supervisor that if it were her life and property at risk from fire, she wouldn't be so quick to judge." His handsome face flushed with anger.

Ashley patted his shoulder. "Stand down, soldier. She's just doing her job. Transporting sick babies is pretty important, too, you know."

Noah chuckled. "Sorry I got riled up. Yes, transporting sick babies and training nurses is very important, and I'm so proud of you."

"Thank you," Ashley said. "So we're all set for the sixteenth through eighteenth?"

"Absolutely! You can count on me. *You have my word.* Nothing will conflict with those dates. I'll put it in my phone calendar right now."

He picked up his phone as his signature ringtone, "Danger Zone," by Kenny Loggins played.

He glanced down at the screen. "Chief Anderson is calling. It must be something important."

*****

Two weeks later, Ashley showered, threw on her scrubs, and rushed out of the house at 6:00 a.m. to make sure everything was ready for her class. The previous night, she had again reminded Noah about the upcoming class and the girls' schedule.

"No worries! I got this! You do what you need to do, and don't worry about a thing."

Even with his reassurance, she was apprehensive. Keeping up with all the household activities wasn't usually on his radar since she was always the one responsible for the girls. *It certainly is his turn to step up to the plate.* Arriving at the hospital, she hurried to arrange what seemed like a million and one details before the students arrived for the workshop.

The day was nonstop with a full class. People had traveled long distances to attend. Ashley gave her maximum effort into providing them with all the information they needed, patiently answering their questions, and mentoring them through the practicum scenarios.

The last student finished her practicum at 1730. It had been a successful but stressful day. Ashley put on her winter coat and headed to her car. The prospect of a delicious hot meal and warm bubble bath awaiting her was very appealing. She'd worked through the lunch break grading exams while munching on a protein bar. Her stomach rumbled.

The next two days would be just as demanding, if not more so. There was a lot of pressure on the attendees to successfully complete the course. Nerves were running high.

Looking forward to the comforts of home, she sighed contentedly, turned on the ignition, and bumped up the heat. The winter sun had already set, and the evening was damp and chilly. She turned on her phone, which had been silenced during the class to avoid interruptions. It immediately started to blow up with multiple missed calls from Emma and Katie.

With shaking hands, she listened to her voice mails as she pulled out of her parking space.

The first message was from Emma. "Mom, it's me. Dad hasn't shown up yet. Everyone's left. Katie and I are the only ones here. We walked to the grocery store and are waiting in front just like you told us. I tried to call him, but he's not picking up either."

She skipped to the next voice mail.

"We've been waiting for Dad for over two hours. It's getting cold and dark. The store closed thirty minutes ago. Nobody's around, and I'm scared. Pick up the phone! Dad isn't answering. Please come and get us!" Katie was whimpering as she ended the call.

Lightning bolts of combined fear and intense anger flooded Ashley's veins. *What is going on?* Surely he didn't forget after all her reminders. Had something happened to him?

She called Emma, reassuring them she was on her way. Breaking the speed limit, she rushed to pick up the girls who were standing in front of the now closed grocery store under the illuminated signage. Their young faces were pale and drawn, and they were shaking with the winter chill and anxiety. White hot rage pulsated through Ashley.

There is no excuse *for this! This is unforgivable!* This couldn't be happening. Double-checking her phone, there were no calls from Noah. She tried to call him, but it went directly to voice mail. The girls huddled into the car, cold and shivering. She cranked up the heater.

"How could he just forget us, Mom?" Katie sobbed.

"Yeah. How could he?" Emma cried.

"Let's not jump to conclusions, girls. There must be something else going on. Let's pray Dad is okay."

She kept her jaw clenched and a white-knuckle grip on the steering wheel all the way home, hoping to hold back all she was thinking from the girls. Pulling into the driveway, she saw the chimney blowing smoke and all the lights on inside. *Hmm. It looks like he's home?*

Noah was settled in his favorite lounge chair, feet propped up. He set his beer down and waved his hand in greeting.

"Hi, girls! How was your day? The 49ers are crushing the Raiders."

"Dad! You *forgot* us! We've been standing in the dark for *hours* waiting for you to pick us up!" Emma sobbed.

Katie chimed in with tears running down her face. "I was so scared and kept trying to call you. How could you *forget* us? I missed my horseback riding lesson!"

"What? Forget you?" Noah stammered, confused. He swept up his phone. Dead. His tanned face blanched as the realization swept through him. "I am *so* sorry! I was wondering where you were. Chief Anderson was alerting me that our statewide team is being activated tomorrow. North winds are kicking up, and the team is set to head out. I completely got sidetracked. I'm so sorry, girls!"

Throwing down her purse and briefcase, Ashley unwound the flannel scarf from her neck and yanked her coat from her arms. "Girls, please feed the animals, then go to your rooms and start homework. I'll call for a pizza."

While they fed the animals, Ashley called in the pizza order. The girls finished their chores and ran upstairs.

Ashley turned to Noah, her voice steely cold, eyes spitting fire. "If something had happened and you were unable to pick up the girls—you could have called me at the hospital. I could have tried to make other arrangements. But *forgetting* to pick up your own children? This...is... *unacceptable!* I ask you *one time* to take responsibility for Emma and Katie, and you failed! Now you're telling me you're leaving tomorrow? You *promised* me this would be your number one priority. Obviously, I can't trust you. How could you do this?" Ashley clenched her fists against her temples, shaking with rage. "I still have two more days of class, and I *told* you how important this commitment is to me and my career!"

Noah tried to put his arms around her, but she slapped his hands away.

"Do *not* touch me! I'm so angry I can't talk to you anymore. Just go and do your macho fire thing!" Stomping into the cold kitchen, she pulled out a bowl and plates. She grabbed a bag of premixed salad and poured the contents in the bowl.

Noah entered the kitchen, his tail between his legs. "I truly am sorry. I'm a moron! But on the bright side, the girls are fine and home safe and sound."

Ashley slammed a handful of silverware on the table. "Do... not...talk...to me."

She was so upset she didn't trust herself to speak. She could not believe he would forget their daughters and leave them in the streets in the cold and dark while he sat watching football and drinking beer.

They could have been assaulted or kidnapped. *He thinks it's fine? Now he's off again for who knows how long, leaving me in the lurch again? I can't do this!*

"You are truly showing what your true priorities are, and apparently, family is not high on the list." Ashley slapped napkins next to the silverware and plates. This was the final nail in the coffin of their relationship. "I do not want to talk to you or even be in the same room with you. Either you or I will sleep on the couch. When you get back, we're going to have a serious discussion about our relationship and family."

Noah tried to give her a hug again. "Babe! What more can I do? I said I was sorry! You're making such a huge deal out of this. You know that when my work calls, I have to go."

Remembering the pinched and scared faces of their daughters standing on the sidewalk in the dark filled Ashley with wrath. She pushed him away, her eyes shooting daggers. "That is precisely one of the items we need to discuss when you get back!" She enunciated each word with a pointy jab of her index finger to his chest.

Noah lifted both hands with a questioning look. "I don't get why you're so upset."

Ashley bit back a scream. "You don't get it! It's what you *don't do*. That's the problem. The fire service loves you and thinks you're wonderful, but your relationship with your family is falling apart. You're so blinded by your work you don't even notice or care." She slapped both hands on his chest and pushed him out of her way. "Give me some space. I'm exhausted and hungry. Now, thanks to you, I need to figure out childcare for the next few days. In case you didn't realize, in addition to keeping this family afloat, I, too, have an important job with a lot of people counting on me to do my best."

The pizza arrived. Ashley grabbed her wallet out of her purse on her way to the door as Noah slunk back into the living room.

14

Ashley tossed and turned all night, still in disbelief that Noah would forget his promise and leave her in yet another bind. Fortunately, she was able to reach her friend, Jackie, who consoled her and agreed to watch the girls and even keep them overnight since Ashley's final day of class started so early. Emma could still go to dance practice, and Jackie's husband would pick her and their daughter up on his way home from work.

Katie was upset that she had missed her riding lesson and would also miss Friday's lesson. Her time at the barn was the highlight of her week. Ashley had promised she would call the riding instructor during her lunch break and try to reschedule the lesson for Saturday. She tried to placate her by agreeing they would spend extra time at the barn Saturday grooming and caring for the horses in addition to her lesson.

Late last night, Ashley had packed lunches and the girls' bags. Noah had promised to drop them off at school this morning on his way out of town.

This morning, he again attempted to apologize and was met with a glacier stare.

"Please, babe. I don't know what else to say. I messed up, and I'm sorry, really sorry."

Ashley grabbed her coat and purse, striding out of the room.

*****

Two long days later, the final student successfully finished her simulation testing. With a wave, Ashley watched her walk proudly out of the classroom with her certificate of completion in hand. Ashley sighed a big breath of relief. Her supervisor had been complimentary of the positive student feedback. This was an important outreach class to the community and was essential to coordination of care in outlying hospitals.

Glancing at her phone, she saw several voice mails from Noah but none from the girls, which was a good sign. She still didn't trust herself to speak civilly, so she was ignoring his calls. It would take a long time, if ever, to get over her frustration and anger. As a mother, she just couldn't fathom how he could *forget* their daughters and then not think it was a big deal. She was also hurt that he had forgotten his promise to have a special dinner awaiting them. All day on Wednesday, she had so been looking forward to quality family time, and instead, it was a disaster. Thinking about it made her feel unimportant and unloved.

Noah knew about her past and issues with abandonment. He knew that making sure their girls were safe and cared for was her number one priority. This was what had sparked such a fire in her the other night. Forgetting to pick up the girls, in her mind, demonstrated a personality flaw in Noah that she was unable to rationalize away.

Ashley packed up her things and walked down the hospital corridor to complete class documentation and then pick up the girls. Tonight, she was treating them to Friday night Chinese takeout. It had been a hard week for them all. And, frankly, she didn't feel like cooking. Remembering her forgotten cell phone in the classroom, Ashley sharply turned around and ran face-to-face into Steve.

"Steve! What are you doing here? I didn't know you were going to be in town."

His face lit up. "Ashley. It's so good to see you! I was asked to consult on a complicated pediatric cardiac surgical case, so I flew up last night."

Leaning toward her, he glanced around to see if anyone was listening. "I saw you walking down the corridor. I wasn't going to say anything, but then you turned around, and here we are. It must be fate." He took her arm and whispered, "Is there anywhere we can talk in private?"

"Yes," Ashley said. "I just finished teaching a three-day workshop and remembered I left my cellphone in the classroom. We can talk in there."

Sitting down across from Ashley, he looked at her affectionately. "I've missed you. How are you doing? Have you come to any decision yet? Not trying to pressure you, but honestly, all I can think about is sharing my life with you."

Ashley raised her head, gazing into Steve's beautiful blue eyes and handsome face. "I've missed you too. I'm close to a decision. Interesting we ran into each other today of all days." Tearfully, she shared the traumatic events of the week.

Steve, too, was stunned that Noah would forget his commitment to care for the girls and was angered as well. "So what are you thinking?"

"I need a little more time and space. I'm still too upset to make a rational decision that changes so many lives." She furrowed her brow. "I think it would be the best if Noah and I legally separate. If he's amenable, we can go for couple's counseling at least to give it our best shot to make it work."

Tears welled in her eyes as she looked up at Steve. "I think I owe that to our almost two decades of building a life together…and also to the girls. Speaking of, I need to go pick them up. I don't want to be late after this week's earlier fiasco. Thank goodness for friends like Jackie and Nick. I don't know what I would do without them."

Steve reached out and caught her hand. "I understand and respect your decision. By the way, Cara and Lexie call your daughters their northern sisters. Isn't that cute? They got along so well."

Ashley laughed. "I've heard mine call your daughters their southern sisters. They tell me they *adopted* each other. Hey, maybe Cara and Lexie would be able to spend some time at our house over Christmas break. The girls would love to take them snowboarding and ice skating. What do you think?"

"That would be amazing," Steve said. "I have the girls during Christmas break, and Stephanie has long-standing plans to go to Europe. I've been asked to speak at the International Pediatric Cardiologist Convention in Atlanta during that time but was just about to tell them I was unavailable because of the girls being with me. Do you think they could visit you then?"

"Absolutely! The northern sisters will be ecstatic!" Glancing at her watch, Ashley frowned. "I'm sorry to cut this short, but I have to jam."

"Understandable. We'll talk and finalize some dates." He brushed a kiss on her cheek, walked to the classroom door, and turned back to wave goodbye.

Ashley rushed back to her office to complete the required paperwork. After scanning the document, she hit the send button to her supervisor and swept out of the hospital to her car. For the first time in weeks, her heart was light. She had a smile on her face, eagerly anticipating the weekend with her daughters and sharing the news of their southern sisters' upcoming visit.

She had not missed Steve's comment that he would have cancelled an important speaking engagement because of his commitment to his daughters. He was a world-renowned pediatric cardiologist on the cutting edge of technology. Publicly sharing his work was critical to his successful career, but he was willing to put that aside for his family. In Ashley's estimation, that spoke volumes about his priorities. She desperately wished Noah shared them.

*****

Ashley exited the hospital as Rodney, the security guard, approached. "Let me walk you to your car."

"Thanks." Shivering in the cold crisp night, she buttoned up her coat and turned up the collar. "Brrr! It does get dark so early this time of year."

Rodney scanned the parking lot as they walked. "Lately, we've had a rash of vehicle break-ins. We think it's people looking for Christmas packages. Make sure you don't leave anything valuable in sight."

"Will do," Ashley agreed as she beeped the lock open on her car. She turned to Rodney and smiled. "Thank you. I appreciate you watching over us."

"You bet. Be careful out there. Lots of crazies around." He shook his head. "Just this week, I was patrolling the parking garage staircase and came across a guy passed out on drugs in the stairwell."

Ashley gasped. "What did you do?"

"I called 911 and administered Narcan. That dude came off his high fast and jumped up like a prize fighter swinging away."

"Oh no! Were you hurt? I've heard people can get really violent when they're administered Narcan and upset because you interrupted their high. Even though they could have died, all they care about are the drugs."

"No, I wasn't hurt. Don't worry about me." Rodney motioned her to get in the car. "It's freezing. Get inside and turn on the heat."

Ashley climbed in and turned on the ignition. "Then what happened?"

"I cuffed him and called for additional security. We were able to hold him down until the police arrived."

"Goodness! I'm glad you weren't hurt."

"Yeah. It's getting worse around here. Employees have been complaining about homeless people wedging their blankets in the front of cars parked in the garage." He shrugged, "Can't say I blame them. They're just trying to protect themselves from the elements."

Ashley reached over and turned up the heater.

Rodney pulled his knit cap down around his ears. "It's tough when they're watching and know people's cars are going to stay put for twelve-hour shifts on a regular basis."

"I hadn't thought about that, but you're right."

"They've even started small fires for warmth and leave piles of ashes and discarded syringes."

"Oh my. Thanks for giving me a heads up. I'll be sure to warn my staff to be extra careful."

"Tell them to request security to walk them to their cars any time they would like. We're a little shorthanded, but I've requested more help from the administration. I requested an enclosed heated golf cart, too, so we can cover more areas quicker." He shook his head despondently. "But I don't know, this new administrator doesn't seem too interested in employee safety."

"Or employee satisfaction," Ashley quipped. "Well, I've gotta go pick up my girls. You stay safe there…and thanks for the escort."

Rodney waved and headed back for another perimeter sweep.

15

In addition to Noah's permanent duty station as air attack officer, seated behind the pilot and directing fighting fire from the air, he was on Statewide Major Incident Command Team Five and qualified for two important positions: air operations and ground operations. There were eight such command teams in the state—four in the north and four in the south.

The teams were composed of twenty-five members. Every member was a specialist in each of the command and support functions. Teams activated for major emergency events whether it be fire, flood, or other disasters and rotated their duty weeks according to a statewide master schedule. Team Four had already been activated this week. Therefore, Team Five was up. The north winds were wreaking havoc, red flag warnings issued for most of the state.

Team Five assembled at the Incident Command Base, waiting for briefing from the first responding officers. Noah's thoughts wandered as he waited for the meeting to begin. *What's going on with Ashley? She hasn't returned any of my calls.* She had been a firefighter's wife long enough to know he had no choice but to go when his team activated.

Only a family emergency or some other major crisis were excusable reasons, and even then, they required a supervisor's permission. Even preapproved vacations necessitated the team member to find a qualified substitute, which was reviewed in advance by the team's Incident Commander.

This was a serious responsibility. Yes, he felt bad about forgetting to pick up the girls, but Ashley overreacted. After all, everything turned out okay. In his estimation, she was way too protective.

He knew she had some childhood issues with abandonment and absent parents, but that was then, and this was now. Ashley had been acting weird ever since returning from the LA trip. She refused all of his advances and was distant and vague about rescheduling their anniversary trip. And now she was saying they needed to have "a serious discussion." Did this have anything to do with Mega Bucks Steve and his fancy jet? Noah's blood ran hot, fists clenching. *If that dude made a move on my wife and family—*

A coworker interrupted his angry thoughts. "Hey, Chief! They're about to start the meeting."

He had difficulty focusing on the briefing as his thoughts kept going back to Ashley and the girls.

"Chief, are you with us? I asked you a question, and you're off in la-la land."

Noah shook his head and rubbed his face. "Sorry, Chief. What was that again?"

The Incident Commander repeated his question. "Did you review the list of ordered resources yet? If so, is it good? Or are you going to need more?"

"No, I haven't had a chance. I'll do it right now."

"Okay, go."

Noah headed to the planning section of the command team and found the latest resource list. Having learned in the briefing that the north winds were greatly going to increase in the next six to eight hours, coupled with low humidity. He rapidly reviewed the list.

To his surprise, few of the requested teams of firefighters were actually going to arrive at this incident. He returned to the briefing, sat down, and raised his hand. When motioned to speak, he stood and addressed the IC, "Chief, I reviewed the resources, and we're very short on firefighters for the next operational period."

The IC shrugged, "Well, I'm not surprised, the entire state is on fire, and resources are stretched thin. Why don't you review which resources can stay on the fire for another twenty-four to thirty-six hours and which we need to pull for safety considerations? Then come back and report to me."

"Will do, Chief." Sitting back down, he fretted.

Noah wasn't going to be popular with the crews no matter what decision was made. He knew just how physically and psychologically tough it was to fight fire day and night for a forty-eight-hour shift and then be told you had to continue for another twenty-four to thirty-six hours.

Noah recalled a fire he had been on as a young firefighter for twenty-one days straight with only a few hours of sleep here and there, under the shade of a tree in a paper sleeping bag. Back then, it being only his second year as a seasonal firefighter, he hadn't packed a go-bag. Twenty-one days with no change of socks or underwear. Hosing each other down to get off some stink. Eating meals ready to eat with tepid water. No coffee, no snacks, no small comforts of civilization.

He remembered cutting line with another firefighter and looking down at his work boot with his ax stuck in it. Both of them were so tired, they acted like they were drunk, laughing and laughing, holding their shaking bellies, tears rolling down their sooty faces. Thank God his boots had steel-tipped toe or he would have been in a world of hurt!

Another time, something like a sharp stick snapped at the back of his calf. He turned to discover a three-foot rattlesnake had bitten through his work boot! Enraged, he ripped the snake off his leg and cut off its head with his ax. Taken off the fire line and transported to the local hospital, he received anti-venom and treatment. After a night's rest, he was cleared and sent back to the fire line.

Over the years, things had gotten better, such as the department renting hotel rooms with private bathrooms and hot showers for the resting crews. On larger fires, the work shifts were twenty-four hours on and twenty-four hours off. However, with big fires burning all over the state and resources stripped, there were no guarantees.

*****

Noah poured over the resource list, identifying what was critical and what could wait to be filled. With high winds quickly approaching, cutting a dozer line around the fast-moving head of a fire was of utmost priority. Once crews could slow or stop the head of the fire, containing the flanks would be the next priority.

Coordinating with air ops would be time-critical while there was still daylight and before the high winds necessitated the aircraft to be grounded for safety. At wind speeds of twenty-plus miles per hour, the air firefighting effort became reduced as the retardant drops lost accuracy. At wind speeds of thirty miles per hour or higher, the aircraft was difficult to control at low altitudes and was unsafe for the pilots. Fortunately, the fire was remote and not currently threatening life or property. However, that scenario could quickly change if the fire shifted direction.

Noah calculated the fire's extent, growth potential, and available resources. It was a huge puzzle with many moving pieces. Thoughts of Ashley and his family back home faded as he focused on the present battle. With a resource assignment plan firmly developed and drafted on paper, he walked to the command center to find the IC. The lack of available resources and changing weather conditions ensured this would be a long hard battle.

As Ground Operations Chief, he had a difficult job to utilize the available resources while protecting the fire crews from harm and saving life and property. He felt the heavy weight of responsibility on his shoulders and sent up a prayer asking for strength, safety, and protection for all.

*****

After putting the girls to bed, Ashley fell to her knees. "Lord, I feel horrible for making Noah sleep on the couch and having an argument with him before he left for a big fire. Please forgive me for my selfishness."

She'd had days to reflect on the events before Noah left. She had come to the conclusion that neither of them had remembered his strike team rotation was up when he agreed to watch the girls. It was so unusual that both team one and team four would be called up on the same week. *I should have made other plans for the girls without involving him. Fire season is always unpredictable, especially the past couple of years.*

"Please help me, Lord, to be more patient and understanding. Please protect him from harm and give him strength for these long difficult days. I know he's exhausted from all these back-to-back fires and certainly doesn't need to come home to all this angst. However, change does need to be made. Please guide me in talking to him with a clear head. Help me make decisions that are your plan and your will and not for my selfish desires. Amen."

Ashley stood up and took several deep cleansing breaths. More at peace, she left the bedroom to rattle some pots and pans for dinner. Emma and Katie had finished their homework and were now playing a board game in front of the fireplace. Both of the girls had been upset by their parents' argument.

"Are you and Daddy getting a divorce?" Katie asked in a quivering voice. "My friend Alice's parents got divorced last year, and she hates it! She and her sister are always going back and forth to their mom's house or their dad's house, and they're always angry and fighting." Her lower lip trembled.

"Katie! That's Mom and Dad's decision, not ours. Dad totally forgot about us and left us on the street in the cold and dark for over two hours, and that is *not* okay." Emma crossed her arms over her chest. "I don't want them to get divorced either, but I want our family to be happy."

Ashley cut in, "Okay, everybody, let's calm down. Nothing is going to be resolved this way. When Dad comes home, we're going to try to work through things. We might need to live in separate homes for a bit while we figure out the future. But you girls are our priority, so please trust us to do what's best for our family."

Katie didn't look consoled, and Emma gave her a reassuring hug. "No matter what, we're sisters."

She hugged her sister back tightly. "Forever. Don't forget that."

"Yes, sisters forever. We stay together."

Ashley's eyes dampened, and her throat clenched. She hated seeing her daughters so worried and unhappy, but she didn't want to give them false hope either.

"I do have some good news! I talked with Steve yesterday, and your southern sisters are going to come stay with us for a couple of days during winter break. How about that?"

"When are they coming? How long can they stay?" Emma asked.

Katie bounced up and down. "Can we take them snowboarding and ice skating?"

"Cara can stay in my room, and Lexie can stay in Katie's!"

Katie nodded her consent. "I want to take Lexie to the barn and show her all my animals. She likes to play with Breyer horses too. We can play stables and build riding arenas and all kinds of cool things."

"Can Cara come to dance class with me?" Emma asked.

Ashley grinned at their enthusiasm. "I think we can do all those things, girls. Once I find out the specific dates, I'll ask for some time off to be available to take you to all these cool places."

"Thanks, Mom! You're the best!"

Bending down to give both girls a hug, she whispered fiercely. "I love you both so much. Don't ever forget that."

"We love you, too, Mom...*and* Dad. We miss him so much. He's never home anymore."

"I know," Ashley said. "All right! Let's move on. I'm going to finish up dinner, and you girls finish your chores, please. Tomorrow is a new day. Let's pack lunches and feed these hungry beasts."

The dogs and Trina clamored around, waiting for their meal.

The girls ran off to do their chores, planning all the fun things they would do when their southern sisters arrived for their visit.

Ashley watched them with a smile on her lips and a happy heart. "Thank you, God, for my precious children. Help me to be a good mom."

Stirring the marinara sauce, she organized her thoughts, preparing for the following day. The cold and flu season was hitting hard, and many nurses were out sick. As happened from time to time, the charge nurses would have to set aside their duties and work in the NICU as staff nurses. Ashley was on the staffing schedule for the next two days in the NICU but was looking forward to it. She loved bedside nursing, especially in the NICU where every shift brought both challenges and rewards.

One of her favorite things was teaching new parents how to feed and care for their little ones, each child such a miracle. Many of them had gone through months and months of being in the NICU. The best days were the ones when a baby finally could go home with their parents.

16

"Morning, girlfriend. How's it going?" Laurie met Ashley in the locker room and gave her a friendly squeeze and then pulled away and did the five-second head-to-toe nursing assessment. She looked at Ashley with concern. "What's wrong, honey?"

At first, Ashley tried to brush off her friend's concerns. "Everything's good. Tired as usual. Noah's still gone and won't be home anytime soon. It's a lot, you know, and here we are at 6:30, taking care of critically ill babies for the next twelve hours."

Laurie shook her head knowingly. "Uh-uh. It's *me* you're talking to. *I see you. I know you.*"

The care and concern in Laurie's voice broke down Ashley's facade. Tears suddenly misted, and her jaw quivered. "Noah and I are going through a rough spot. I don't know if we're going to make it."

Laurie pulled her in for a tight embrace. "Okay, now I get it. I got your back. Let's see if we can work in the same section and take our lunch breaks together. And we can talk."

Ashley smiled through her tears as other day shift staff entered the locker room. "Thanks, that sounds great. But for now, I need to pull it together."

Laurie nodded reassuringly. "Love you, girl."

They walked out of the locker room and into the NICU filled with a cacophony of bells and alarms. Grabbing clean cover gowns, they started their mandatory five-minute scrub. Laurie glanced at the assignment sheet over the sink. "Hey, Ashley, we're not in the same section. Also, Tamera is scheduled to work with you."

Tamera, a new graduate, was going through orientation. The process for NICU was extensive, given the complexity and intensity of care. It was mandatory for NICU nurses to have advanced skills, particularly in the area of assessing their patients for the minutest of changes, which could signal a downward spiral.

Walking into their assigned area, Tamera turned and faced Ashley. "Thanks for orienting with me. You're always so calm and professional."

Ashley blushed. "Thanks. You're making good progress. Looks like we're assigned to some very unstable preemies. We'll work especially on your assessment skills today."

"Sounds good. I know how critical that is."

The NICU became an extension of the mother after an infant's delivery, providing all the necessary nutrients, oxygen, and warmth the placenta and uterus supplied in utero. Neonatal nurses were known to be territorial, there to protect and nourish their fragile patients just like a mother.

The Level III NICU was a buzzing beehive of activity with doctors, nurses, respiratory therapists, x-ray and lab technicians, registered dietitians, housekeeping, and all the other support personnel required to maintain the neonates' care.

Parents were allowed at the bedside 24-7, except during report or an adverse event such as a Code Blue.

During morning report, she was approached by a nursing instructor from the local university. "Hey, Ashley, this is Victoria Langley. Would you mind mentoring her from 7:30–2:30 today and tomorrow? She's one of my sharpest students this semester and is thinking she would like to eventually work in the NICU."

Knowing a lot of the nurses didn't like to mentor students, as it was a lot of extra work, she agreed. "Of course, be happy too." *Everyone deserves a chance. We were all new nurses in the beginning.*

The combination of mentoring a new employee and having a student was a lot to ask, but she was agreeable and looking forward to providing a good learning experience.

The instructor showed Victoria how to scrub in and put on her protective cover gown. Once these steps were completed, the eager nursing student bounded to Ashley's side and stuck like glue.

"Hi, Victoria. I'm Ashley, and this is Tamera. She's just been hired and is in orientation." Ashley turned to face Victoria directly. "The NICU is extremely specialized. These next two days that you're assigned with me will be observational, meaning very little, if any, hands on."

Victoria solemnly nodded.

Ashley continued, "In reality, it takes at least two years of intense training for an RN to become a seasoned NICU nurse. It's very important that you don't touch any of the settings on the pumps, warming table, or ventilator." She made eye contact to make sure Victoria was paying attention. "These micro preemies are extremely fragile. We make teeny, tiny adjustments to any of the equipment settings and then closely monitor their responses."

"Yes, ma'am." Victoria turned, bumping her elbow into the side of the warming table. The baby had a startled reflex followed by a drop in oxygenation levels. "Oops! So sorry!"

Ashley turned up the baby's oxygen. "It's important to make slow thoughtful movements. There are a lot of people, equipment, and moving pieces in the NICU." She scooted a chair against the wall. "Why don't you have a seat here and just observe for now. It's going to get very busy in here shortly."

Victoria meekly perched up on the stool with huge eyes, taking in all the action.

Tamera glanced over at the nursing student, smiling sympathetically. "You're okay, kiddo. I was there just a few years ago. You'll learn a ton just from observing. I promise."

"Thanks. I feel so useless just sitting here."

Ashley smiled at both of them. "When report is over, let's go over the 0800 assessments together. That'll be a good learning experience. I'll try to explain as much as possible, but if it gets crazy, you'll have to just observe. Okay?"

"Uh, Ashley, can you come over here?" Tamera's voice was tense and strained.

Ashley hurried to her side. With a practiced professional eye, she scanned the alarming monitors, visually assessing the neonate in the warming table, hooked up to various tubes and monitors.

"CO_2 levels are rising, and oxygenation is dropping fast," Tamera reported. "I'm hearing decreased breath sounds on the right. I think we might have a pneumothorax. The last x-ray showed a weakness on the right lower lung, and I think it collapsed."

Ashley whipped out her stethoscope and listened to the baby's lungs. "I concur. Good call, Tamera. What do you recommend we do for our next step?"

"Order a STAT chest x-ray and arterial blood gas and notify the respiratory therapist and the covering doctor or nurse practitioner."

Ashley nodded affirmatively. Tamera waved to Nick, the section's assigned RT, and motioned him to the bedside. "It looks like we have a pneumo here."

Nick listened to the baby's breath sounds while scanning the monitors. The x-ray technician scurried over with the portable x-ray machine. Lab showed up at the bedside and, with a nod to go ahead from Tamera, drew the arterial blood gas from the umbilical artery catheter. The scenario ran like clockwork.

The NICU was designed to act immediately in events when STAT testing was needed. They always had several lab techs and a portable x-ray machine with a technician available around the clock. In less than a minute, the NICU nurse practitioner was at the bedside concurring with the suspected diagnosis. Nick was already hand-ventilating the baby's endotracheal tube in order to provide more oxygen and decrease the buildup of hazardous carbon dioxide.

The covering medical provider on call, Kelly, a NICU nurse practitioner, called out orders. "Tamera, set up a needle aspiration kit. Then call the surgeon to insert a chest tube. Set up the chest tube for negative pressure at ten millimeters of mercury."

"Got it." Tamera pulled on her sterile gloves and handed the long needle to the NICU NP.

Upon inserting the needle into the lower right lung lobe and aspirating air that had collected outside the lung, the air inside the lung expanded, and the oxygen level started to improve. Shortly, the surgeon arrived and inserted a chest tube to maintain the lung's expansion at the bedside. The baby's vital signs continued to stabilize. Nick slowed down the hand ventilation, gradually able to put the baby back on the manual ventilator.

He called out to the team, "Repeat blood gases and x-rays are now showing normal lung inflation and ventilation."

"Great job, everyone!" Ashley congratulated her peers. "Tamera, fantastic assessment skills and identifying the problem early."

Tamera flushed under Ashley's praise. "Thank you for letting me handle it and not taking over. I appreciate you letting me gain the experience."

"Well, that's how you learn. Right?" Patting Tamera on the back, Ashley turned to Victoria, sitting on the stool with wide eyes.

"Wow! That was awesome. I can see why you warned me to stay put. I've never seen such a quick response with so many people at one time. You guys were incredible. I want to be a NICU nurse."

Ashley chuckled. "All in a day's work. That's why I love my job."

*****

Later, sitting in a quiet corner on her lunch break with Laurie, she tearfully shared her concerns with her friend. "I've spent a lot of time in prayer about our marriage. I don't see anything changing in the near future unless Noah quits his job or I do, which isn't going to happen."

Laurie softly rubbed her back, trying to console her best friend.

Ashley took a ragged breath. "What hurts the most is that he just doesn't get it or even *try* to understand how his behavior affects our marriage and family." She wiped her eyes with a tissue. "I think the next step is for Noah to move out."

17

⌘

Several more weeks went by with Noah still on the fire. Ashley was preparing dinner for the girls and herself when she heard Noah's ringtone. She picked up the phone to see that it was a video call. With a dry swallow, she swiped answer. His tanned weathered face appeared on the screen, eyes rimmed with red. He looked spent.

"Hi, Ash, how is everybody? It's still blowing and going here."

"Yeah, I've been watching the coverage on the news. Everything's so bone-dry, and the winds! Looks terrifying." She gripped the phone with two hands. "Please be careful out there. I saw that several more firefighters were injured."

"Not going to lie. It's bad…and no end in sight. Four firefighters were injured on a canyon wall. Two others killed. The firestorm came whipping up the canyon and formed a fire tornado. Poor guys had no chance to shelter." He cleared his throat roughly. "Sorry, it's just so smoky. I probably drink two gallons of water during a shift but still feel dehydrated."

Ashley felt powerless and fretful. "Please be extra careful, and don't forget your electrolyte tablets."

"I ran out a couple of days ago. Been drinking that sports drink with electrolytes."

"Are you watching your urinary output for dehydration? What color is your urine?"

Laugh lines appeared on his soot-stained face. "Nurse Ashley, I'm a big boy. We don't need to discuss my urinary output."

"Sorry about that. My control freak nurse alter ego popped out."

"At least you care about my hydration."

"We *all* care, Noah. Let me get the girls. They've been want-ing to talk to you." Walking to the foot of the stairs, she called out, "Emma, Katie, Dad's on the phone." She turned back to the screen as the girls thundered down the stairs. "I'm going to finish making dinner while you talk to the girls. Bye now. Be safe. Oh, and by the way, happy anniversary."

"Oops, sorry babe. The days just run into each other on the fire line. Happy anniversary. I'll make it up to you. Bye. Love you!"

Ashley didn't reply but handed the phone to the girls.

*****

Two weeks later, it appeared that staffing releases from the fire might begin shortly. Ashley hoped Noah would be home before Thanksgiving, but nothing was a guarantee. His team was one of the first on the long string of fires and therefore would be among the first to be released.

Noah's family was planning a huge celebration, as usual. It was always a massive occasion, starting with the traditional Turkey Trot Jog/Walk-a-thon supporting a local community cause, followed by preparing, cooking, and serving hundreds of meals to the homeless and underserved. Meanwhile, Noah's mom, Mary, would be bustling in the kitchen with her daughters and daughters-in-law, helping to prepare a huge family feast.

Normally, Ashley looked forward to the holiday for weeks. This year was different. She knew the girls were excitedly anticipating see-ing their cousins. Holidays were full of childhood fun and making memories for years to come.

After dinner and dishes, the girls were upstairs finishing home-work while Ashley sat in the living room with a cup of tea, remi-niscing. Her childhood memories were quite different from Noah's. Her parents lived in a mini mansion in a gated community. Ashley's father, Harold Bowman, was a renowned personal injury attorney, and her mother, Adrianna, a career socialite, was consumed by com-munity volunteer work. Her mom was always busy attending this or that function, lunches, and fundraising engagements. She thrived on it, spending considerable time and money on her outfits and jewelry to maintain the image of a successful trophy wife.

Ashley remembered one of many arguments they had when she was a girl.

Walking into her parents' bedroom, she found her mother sorting through her evening dresses. "Mom, can Susan come over after school on Friday and spend the night?"

Her mother turned with a terse tight-lipped expression. "I already told you we have the gala event on Friday. You can stay at her house if her mom or dad will pick you up and bring you home on Saturday." Examining her fingernails, she turned back to her dresses. "You know we always play golf on the weekends."

Ashley pouted. "You never let me have any friends over."

"Quit complaining! You don't know how good you have it. Now here's some money. Go order a pizza for your dinner. Your father and I are going out."

Her lower lip quivered. "Can't I come? I don't want to be left alone again. I get scared when I'm all by myself."

"*Grow up!* You're almost ten. Dad and I have plans with our friends." Her mother stiffly walked away.

Spending many lonely nights hiding under the covers, shaking with fear as the night noises loomed threatening in the cavernous house, she longed for company, another warm body. She had begged her parents for a kitten, but they always refused.

"They're too messy with the litter box and everything. Ick!"

"But I'll take care of it," Ashley pleaded. "You won't have to do anything. I'll use my birthday and chore money to buy food and cat litter. Please?"

"The answer is no. Now stop bugging us."

Dejected, Ashley crept back into her isolated room to read and get lost in the world of words. The message she repeatedly received from her parents came through loud and clear. *We really don't care about what you want...or your feelings.*

Several months later, Ashley found a stray cat in their backyard. Secretly, she fed it leftovers and set a pan of water under the back stairs. She named it Tigger because of its tiger-like stripes. First thing when she came home from school, she would call Tigger's name, smiling as the cat would peek out from under the steps and jump into her lap, purring. She would brush him and play with him for hours after school. Tigger was her only friend, her everything.

One stormy night, her parents out at another dinner party, she snuck him into her room. The thunder rumbled, but holding him close, she relaxed. Tigger purred, kneading biscuits. Ashley fell fast asleep to the peaceful sound.

Her mother's shrill voice jolted her awake. "What have you been thinking, Ashley? Those things have germs and fleas. Yuck!"

"But, Mom—" Tears filled Ashley's eyes. "I love Tigger, and he loves me. Please?"

"Absolutely not. Take it outside this instant."

"But, Mom, its cold and rainy outside. Please. Can't he stay inside just tonight?"

"I said no. Do what you're told. *Now!*"

Reluctantly, Ashley obeyed, but resentment built. She continued to play with Tigger outside after school and on weekends. She fed him and brushed him. His favorite toys were feathers and long pieces of dry grass she would tease him with. He would settle in her lap as she stroked his silky fur, purring contentedly. She couldn't understand why her mother was so against having an indoor cat. But then she realized her mother didn't want to be bothered with anything other than herself.

One night, weeks later, she heard a cat fight during the night. Flinging open the patio door, she called over and over. "Tigger! Tigger! Come here."

"Ashley! What are you doing?" Her mother grabbed her shoulder roughly and pulled her inside, slamming and locking the door.

"Mom," Ashley pleaded. "It's Tigger! He needs help!"

"This is exactly why I didn't want that thing inside. They're wild animals. Now go back to bed." Her mother crossly pulled the patio curtains shut.

Huddling under the covers, Ashley cried. The horrific screeching noises continued. She knew it was Tigger. After what seemed like forever, the noises faded, and she finally drifted off into a restless nightmare-filled sleep.

The next day, she searched for hours, finally finding Tigger, lifeless in a bloody heap of torn fur. Hot bitter tears of anger and grief flooded her young cheeks. She despised her mother for not letting Tigger be safe inside at night. This was *her* fault. Tigger wasn't just some flea-bitten animal. He was her companion, her friend.

She wrapped his body in a bath towel and dug a grave. Marking it with a cross made of twigs, she vowed that someday when she grew up, she would have a household of pets. She would love them and care for them.

Many years later, when Ashley had just graduated from high school, the doorbell rang late one summer night, startling her out of a deep sleep. Slipping her arms into her bathrobe, she stumbled sleepily to the front door and turned on the porch light. She peered through the peephole and saw two uniformed officers standing outside.

One officer called out while both of them held up their police IDs for her to see. "Miss Bowman. I'm Officer Murray, and this is Officer Connor from the Highway Patrol. Can we talk with you?"

With shaking hands, Ashley unlatched the deadbolt and opened the door. She tightened her robe as they entered the foyer. Flicking on lights, she gestured them into the living room.

"Please sit down." She waved at the couch.

They sat on the edge, serious expressions on their faces.

Officer Murray cleared his throat. "Miss Bowman? Is there anyone else here with you tonight?"

She shook her head. "No. Just me."

"How old are you?"

"Eighteen. Why are you asking all these questions?"

The officers shared a glance. After a pause, Officer Murray answered. "Miss Bowman."

"Call me Ashley."

"Ashley." He took a breath and clasped his hands in front of him. "I'm very sorry to inform you that your parents, Mr. and Mrs. Bowman, died tonight in a car accident."

Her eyes widened as her hand flew up to cover her mouth. "How? I mean, what happened? Are you...sure?"

"We just came from the scene. Their car crossed the double yellow line in front of a semi."

Ashley clasped her hands over her face, tears streaming down her cheeks.

The officers gave her a few minutes to process the information. "We're terribly sorry to have to give you this news. Do you have anyone you can call to come over and stay with you?"

She shook her head and wiped her tears. "Nope. It's just me." She sobbed. "It's always been just me."

The officers shared a frown of concern.

With a wave of her hand, she continued in a shaky voice. "My parents were probably on their way home from another party. All my life it's been this party or that function. I'm used to being alone. I bet they had one too many martinis and then got behind the wheel." She let out a heavy exhale. "Was anyone else hurt?"

Officer Conner shook his head. "No. The truck driver is okay. There weren't any other vehicles involved. Again, we're so sorry to have to give you this news."

Ashley stood up, a few tears trickling down her face. "I'm glad to hear no one else was hurt. I'll be okay."

"Again. Our condolences." He handed her his business card. "Please call this number if you need anything." He scanned her face. "Do you have a friend or a neighbor who could stay with you for a few days?"

Wiping her eyes and nose, Ashley sniffed. "No. I'll be fine. I'm used to being alone."

"Please do call if you need anything." Officer Murray patted her back gently. "There are people here to help. Just reach out, okay? I'll have the social worker get in touch with you tomorrow if that's all right."

"All right," Ashley forlornly agreed. "Goodnight."

She closed the door, bolted it, and turned off the lights. Climbing back into bed, she curled into a fetal position. Now more than ever, she felt utterly alone.

18

Later that night, after tucking the girls in bed with a hug and a kiss, Ashley crawled into bed and pulled the covers wearily over her shoulders. Gazing at the ceiling, sleep evaded her as it had so often in the recent weeks.

She thought about the upcoming holidays. She didn't have family to spend the holidays with other than Noah's. After her parents died, the rest of her extended family didn't stay in touch. She loved his family, but this year, she didn't have the energy to put on a smiling face. At least if Noah was with them, it would be easier than if it was just her and the girls.

She also knew she couldn't hide her feelings well. Her face was an open book, and her mother-in-law was very astute. She could read Ashley from a mile away.

She let out a heavy sigh and thought to herself, *I just can't deal with all of this right now.* Closing her eyes, they felt gritty and raw. She let her thoughts swirl around her impending discussion with Noah about him moving out. She knew he would be furious, and she wasn't looking forward to the conversation. Hearing a chirp from her phone, she looked at the screen. It was Noah. "I'll be home by 5:30 tomorrow night. Can't wait to see you all! Xoxox!"

*****

"I'm home!" Noah enthusiastically shouted from front entrance. "Anyone here?"

Within moments, the dogs came rushing to meet him, followed by the girls and Trina. There was a flurry of hugs and enthusiastic barking. Nikki and Callie were beside themselves, leaping up on him, excited to have one of their favorite people back home.

Trina joined the welcoming party, arching against his legs and swishing her tail. Reaching up with her two front legs, she stood on her hind legs, pawing the air as if to say, "Pick me up."

Laughing, Noah tried to return hugs from the girls, pet the dogs, and pick up Trina all at the same time. "It's so good to be home. You girls grew while I was gone. How is everyone? I want to hear all about school and your activities."

Stepping into the kitchen, Noah glanced around the room. "Where's Mom?"

Emma gave him another tight hug. "I think she's in your room."

Ashley took a deep breath and walked into the kitchen. "I'm right here. Hey, Noah. Glad to see you back safe and sound."

Walking over to her husband, she noticed the deep bags under his eyes, several weeks' growth of beard, and gaunt cheeks. The stress of the past weeks had taken its toll. Now was not the time to dive into a deep relationship discussion. He needed some time to recharge his batteries, get adequate sleep, nourishing food, and enjoy the comforts of home.

She reached up to give him a side hug. "How about some carb loading tonight? Spaghetti, salad, and garlic bread sound good?"

Noah shrugged. "Anything you make sounds great, babe. I've been dreaming about your home-cooking. Let me grab my gear out of the car and then wash off this filth. I'm going to throw away these clothes. They're beyond cleaning."

"No argument from me." Ashley laughed. "I'll bring you a garbage bag." Taking a whiff of him, she scrunched up her nose. "Maybe you can undress in the garage."

Noah chuckled. "That bad, huh? I can't even smell myself anymore after all these weeks on the fire."

With a sigh, Noah looked at his family. "It's so wonderful to see my girls. I missed you all so much."

Ashley smiled softly. "We missed you, too, and we're thankful you're home, safe and sound. There's a lot to share with you and important things to discuss. But for now, shower and relax. Dinner will be ready in about half an hour."

*****

Noah chewed on Ashley's "important things to discuss" as he dragged his gear out of his fire vehicle. *She's not still dwelling on me forgetting to pick up the girls at school while she was teaching that class, is she? I thought for sure she would be over that by now.* Rolling his neck to relieve built up tension, he dropped his filthy gear on the garage floor to deal with later and stripped down to his skivvies, tossing his disgustingly filthy clothes in the garbage bag Ashley had provided.

Ashley looked drawn and fatigued. There wasn't much of a homecoming welcome from her, just a side hug like you would give an acquaintance. No lip-searing kiss like in the past. As he trudged down the hallway to the master bathroom, his happiness at finally being home was replaced with concern at what the future held for their family.

*****

The evening passed uneventfully. Noah was so exhausted after being able to let his guard down that he fell fast asleep in the recliner after dinner. Ashley could hear his snores from the kitchen as she stacked the dishwasher.

She smiled at Emma and Katie. "Thanks for your help, girls. Why don't you finish your homework and get ready for the school week? Emma, make sure your dance tights are clean for tomorrow, and both of you pack your backpacks. Okay? I work a twelve-hour shift tomorrow, but Dad will be home. Remember, he said he would take you to school and pick you up afterward to take you to your lessons."

Emma scowled. "Yeah, he *said* he would...but will he really?"

"Yeah," Katie chimed in. "I don't want to be forgotten...again."

Ashley took a breath before answering. *Lord, are my words and actions affecting the girls' responses? If so, please forgive me, and help me be a better role model.*

She smiled at both of the girls. "Let's have some grace here. Dad loves you, and he has a challenging and dangerous job. He feels terrible about what happened. I'm positive it will never happen again."

At least, I sincerely hope not.

She shooed them away. "Now scat! Go get ready for tomorrow."

Emma put a shush finger to her mouth as they tiptoed around their sleeping father and up the stairs to their rooms with Callie and Nikki following. Trina was curled up on Noah's chest, contentedly purring.

Ashley turned inward to her spiraling thoughts as she prepped the coffee maker for the morning and packed her and the girls' lunches. Stepping lightly, she switched off lights and closed the door to their bedroom. She turned on the bathwater, laid out her work uniform for tomorrow, and packed her work bag. Sinking into the steaming bubbles, she let out a yawn. She was thankful Noah and his crew were home safely and also thankful Noah was sound asleep in the other room.

Soon they would need to have a serious discussion, but now was not the time. They were all exhausted. Ashley needed to have some prayerful discussions with the Lord and prepare her words. She loved Noah and always would. He was a wonderful man and father. It was hard for her to imagine all the responsibilities he carried on his shoulders, and he couldn't imagine all of hers. She wished they could be a couple and family like they once were. She hated that the girls had lost trust in him and felt tinges of shame that she had verbalized that distrust perhaps a few too many times. *That's why God gave us two ears...and one mouth.*

*****

The next day at work, Ashley was assigned to the same section and again orienting with Tamera, who was adjusting nicely to the demands of the NICU and already demonstrating excellent priority-setting skills. Ashley had also agreed to mentor Victoria for a second day. After reminding Victoria to observe and use careful purposeful movements, she turned to Tamera.

"Okay, let's go over your 0800 assessments and review labs before morning rounds." She motioned for Victoria to come closer and listen as they reviewed the four neonates in their section.

"Let's look at the electrolyte panel. Hmm, baby Jackson's potassium is borderline low, and his sodium levels a tad high. What do you think, Tamera?" Ashley clicked her pen top.

"Well, the docs might want to consider taking the baby off the dextrose sodium chloride drip and instead run hyper-alimentation solution." She turned to Victoria. "After a few weeks, when things stabilize, and a neonate is on an IV solution with sugar and electrolytes only, their bodies eventually need protein and lipids in order to maintain growth requirements. That's when we administer a specially prepared IV solution that contains protein, dextrose, and electrolytes. IV lipids or fats are also administered but in a separate IV line as they don't mix well. Often, supplemental potassium is added to maintain the stability of the electrolytes."

"Good explanation." Ashley clapped Tamera on the back.

"Now I have a question for you." She smiled at Victoria. "Can you tell me what the electrolyte potassium does for the body and what the normal potassium blood level is?"

"I know this one. We covered fluids and electrolytes in our last few lectures." She tapped her finger to her forehead. "Potassium is both a mineral and an electrolyte. It helps nerves to function properly and muscles to contract. It's important in regulating the heart rate and—drum roll please—low potassium levels can cause fatigue and abnormal heart rhythms. The normal lab levels are 3.6–5.2 millimoles per liter," she proudly concluded.

"Excellent!" Ashley exclaimed. "You receive an A+ for the day."

Beaming, Victoria playfully patted herself on the shoulder. "I've told the other students how awesome you are, Ashley. They're all going to request you for their NICU rotation."

She blushed. "So kind of you to say, but I don't always work directly in the unit. I'm a supervisor, so I have other responsibilities."

Tamera piped up, "I agree with Victoria. You're the best mentor, so calm and thorough. You never make me feel stupid, and I learn a ton every time we work together. Have you ever considered becoming a nursing instructor? You would be fantastic."

"Wow, guys, thanks for all the kudos. You're making my day."

It would be an interesting challenge. Maybe something to think about for the future. I would have to go back to school for my master's degree. No, I can't do that. I can barely get through each day as it is with all the girls' activities and the craziness of fire season. Especially now, with our relationship falling apart. Maybe when they're older. Food for thought.

Later, on her break, she checked her phone for messages. There was a text from Noah: "Sorry I conked out in the chair. I slept so hard I woke up in the same position. I would have preferred holding you in my arms."

Ashley inwardly cringed at how she most likely would have pushed him away.

"Just to reassure you, the girls made it to school on time, and I'll be picking them up and taking them to their after-school activities as promised. Also, you will have a nice hot dinner waiting for you when you get home. I love you so much and hope your day is going well. Looking forward to seeing you tonight."

He was trying, but it was going to take a lot more than promises this time. The door to the break room opened, and the pleasant face of her supervisor, Michelle, appeared.

"Hi, Ashley. They told me you were probably in here. Can I speak with you in my office? I told Tamera you might be delayed for a few minutes, and she's fine. The charge nurse will cover while you're gone."

What's going on? Ashley followed Michelle to her office and settled in the chair across from her.

The office was decorated with inviting cushy pillows and colorful plants. She smiled at the rustic wooden plaque with the words of Aibileen Clark from one of Ashley's favorite movies, *The Help.*

"You is kind, you is smart, you is important"—Ashley often said these words to her daughters as a positive affirmation. They would smile back at their mom, roll their eyes at her, and say, "You are too."

Michelle folded her hands. "I wanted a chance to touch base with you about a couple of items and also check in and ask how you're doing. I know this has been a brutal fire season. Is Noah home yet? Last time we talked, he had been assigned to a large fire for weeks. I watch the news and see home after home destroyed. It must be stressful for you. How are the girls?"

Ashley tried to keep her emotions in check, not wanting to open the floodgates into a full-on ugly cry. Michelle's kind, sympathetic face was her undoing, and the tears began to flow. She sobbed with shuddering heaving shoulders and sniffling gasps. Oh no, the ugly cry! She couldn't believe she was breaking down this way, but once she started, she couldn't stop.

Michelle came around the desk and patted her back. "All right, let it out."

Ashley continued to sob for several minutes until she was able to gain control.

Michelle handed her a box of tissues. "Take your time, Ashley. There's a lot of emotion and stress stored. It's cathartic to let it out."

Ashley dabbed at her eyes and blew her nose. "Thank you. I guess I had built up quite a few walls that needed to come down. Yes, it's been really tough. I worry about Noah and his crew's safety constantly. I watch the news, too, and have seen how the fires are destroying life and property. There doesn't seem to be an end in sight. I'm trying to hold it together for the girls, but frankly, our marriage is in trouble."

Ashley inhaled deeply and exhaled. "As my supervisor, you don't need to know all this, but I know I can trust you. I haven't discussed this with anyone other than Laurie. Anything you say to me is always confidential. Thank you for trusting me enough to share your troubles. I could tell you weren't your usual bubbly cheerful self, but I wasn't sure if it was the horrific fire season or something else. Please let me know if I can help in any way."

"Thank you." Ashley wiped her eyes and blew her nose one last time. "First the ugly cry, and now I have to return to the unit looking like a mess."

Michelle laid her hand on top of Ashley's for a second. "You'll be fine. I wanted to pass on some compliments from the nursing instructors to you. Several of them took the time to shoot me an e-mail or stop by my office. The nursing students are raving about what a great experience they're having with you in the NICU. You have become quite sought-after, and I want you to know how much I appreciate your efforts.

"I know a lot of the nurses don't want to precept students, and it's an extra responsibility on top of orienting new employees, which, by the way, you excel in that role as well. Honestly, Ashley, you have a special gift in education and developing staff. I've been thinking about how we could incorporate an educator position with your supervisory duties, but I think it might be too much on your plate right now. However, I went to the hospital board, and they would be willing to fund your master's degree if you signed a contract to stay with the hospital in an educator role for a minimum of two years."

Ashley sat back in her chair and took a deep breath. "Wow. That's an amazing opportunity that I will give some prayerful consideration. It's funny. I was just thinking about getting my master's degree earlier today but thought I would need to wait until the girls are more independent. Now, with the situation with Noah and myself, everything will have to go on the back burner." Taking another shuddering breath, she mentally shored her emotions.

"Take your time to think about it. There's no rush. Maybe after the holidays we can discuss it further." Michelle nodded encouragingly. "Speaking of the holidays, we're short on nursing staff. Do you have plans? Or are you available to work? I hate to ask, but we're desperate for staffing. I also need to staff transport teams. The last few schedules, you were unavailable because of Noah's work and your responsibilities with the girls."

Michelle leaned forward, placing her hand reassuringly on Ashley's shoulder. "I know a lot of things are out of your control right now, but you also know it's a requirement to transport at least twice quarterly to qualify for the team. I've been ignoring that for the last few quarters because you're such a wonderful asset to the team, but that can't continue for much longer. People notice, and there's already been some grumbling from nurses who want to join the transport team."

Ashley massaged her temples with her fingertips. Taking a swig from her water bottle, she fought an internal war with conflicting emotions. Her worry about the girls and Noah's schedule fought with her desire to stay on the transport team and have her career be as important as Noah's. The NICU transport team was a highly sought-after position and one she had worked very hard to attain. Why should she be always the one to acquiesce? Because she was a woman and a mom? It wasn't fair.

"Noah is supposed to be off for Thanksgiving, but that's no guarantee with fire season the way it is. We usually go to his parents. There's a ton of family, and the girls love playing with their cousins." Ashley made up her mind on the spot. "Put me on the schedule. As many transport team and regular shifts as you need to fill. If Noah is called on a fire, I'll ask his mom to take the girls. She would love to watch them and frequently offers to. It's a bit of a drive there and back for short notice, but with planning, I can take them on my day off, and they can stay for the week."

Michelle nodded. "Yes. That will work great and certainly solves a big headache for me, but what about you? What about your Thanksgiving celebration?"

Ashley shrugged. "No worries. It'll be a nice break being on my own without worrying about Noah and the girls." *And I don't want to face everyone this year. They would see through my facade in a heartbeat, and I hate to disappoint them. They always comment on what a fairy tale love story we are…well, we used to be.*

After her conversation with Michelle, Ashley made a quick pit stop to splash some water on her face and touch up her lip gloss. She saw most of the remnants of her break down had resolved. No one would see her recent tears unless they looked closely, and most people don't. She headed back into the noisy NICU and was swept up in the tasks of the day.

After giving report to the night shift nurse, she walked to her car accompanied by the ever-watchful security guide, Rodney, and drove home, heavy in thought over her meeting with Michelle. *Master's degree in nursing, huh?* It was amazing the hospital was willing to subsidize her education. Doubts circled her mind as she pondered how she could work full-time and be an active and present mom and wife. *Well, the wife part might not be an issue soon.*

19

Dinner was delicious. It was wonderful to come home to a hot meal with her family. Noah shooed her away from the table. "I got this. Go take a nice bubble bath. The girls finished their homework, lunches prepped, and animals fed. Relax. We're going to play some board games and then off to bed. It's a school night."

"Thank you." Ashley gave him an appreciative smile. "Dinner was great, and I'm exhausted."

Sensing her inner turmoil but not realizing the extent of it, Noah offered to sleep in the guest room. "You're tired, and frankly, I'm still recovering from some long days and nights."

He did look haggard. He had lost weight and, despite the shower and shave, still looked like he had been dragged through a knothole.

This was unusual for Noah. Normally, he would bounce right back after a fire siege. Walking down the hallway to the bedroom, she worried. *It's my fault, all this drama and tension at home.* A little voice inside her head hissed, *But you weren't the one who forgot the girls in the cold and dark. Your work is as important as his, and you deserve to be happy and not worry all the time. Steve wouldn't make all these demands on you.* She appreciated Noah's efforts and knew he was trying to make up. Unfortunately, their issues ran deeper than a dinner, cleanup, and packed lunches could fix.

Throwing her scrubs into the laundry basket, she stepped into the bathroom to soak the day's troubles away. Despite the long workday and fatigue, she couldn't keep her mind from spiraling. Was she making a huge mistake by telling Noah she wanted a separation? Would she and the girls be better off with Steve and his family? *Who do I really want to spend the rest of my life with? Are things ever going to change with Noah's job and fire season? Or is this going to go on and on? Does he even care or realize what it's doing to all of us?*

With a heavy heart, she stepped out of the tub, toweled off, and finished getting ready for bed. Her thoughts turned toward tomorrow. They needed to have the discussion, and she was dreading it.

Sleep was elusive. Restless, she tossed and turned. The night slowly dragged on as what-ifs, should haves, and doubts amplified in her head. A tearful prayer to God asking for rest and peace seemed to go unanswered. Ashley kept pushing rest and peace aside and reaching to tug on her fears and anxieties.

The following morning, Noah stepped into the kitchen, wet hair fresh from the shower. "Hey, I know you're off work today. Why don't I take the girls to school this morning?"

"That would be great," Ashley said. "I've got a ton of housework and laundry to catch up on."

"Or," Noah suggested, "we could both go to drop them off and then you, and I could grab breakfast at Two Chicks and a Yolk. You mentioned there were some things you wanted to discuss, and we could combine that with breakfast. Then I can help with the chores when we get back."

"Oh, no," Ashley hastily replied, "we need to have a *private* discussion."

Noah wrinkled his brow. "That sounds pretty serious. I guess I'll be back shortly." Grabbing the car key from the key holder, he turned and called upstairs, "Time to bug out, girls."

*****

Thirty minutes later, he was back. Ashley took a jagged breath, steeling herself for the upcoming life-changing discussion. Noah took a seat in the recliner across from hers.

He tented his fingers and leaned forward. "Okay, babe. Let's discuss what's on your mind. Are you still upset about me forgetting to pick up the girls?"

Ashley nodded.

An angry scowl crossed his face, and he threw up his arms in exasperation. "I apologized to you over and over about that. I'm truly sorry, and it won't happen again. End of story." Fisting his hands together, he scooted forward in his chair. "Next item?"

Hearing his angry tone, the dogs came running into the room, barking loudly.

Ashley hated it when he used that patronizing tone. She brushed a lock of hair from her face with trembling fingers and dropped the bombshell. "It runs much deeper than that Noah. Our marriage is failing, and our family is suffering because of it. We can't go on the way things are."

Her fingernails dug into her palms as she willed herself not to cry and to stand firm. "I want a legal separation, and I think we should see a marriage counselor. I feel we owe it to our fifteen-year marriage and the girls to see if we can salvage what's left."

*****

A flood of feelings swept through Noah—surprise, shock, sadness, and finally white-hot anger.

He slammed his open palm on the coffee table, his muscles tense and as his arms corded with rage. "It's that Steve guy, isn't it? I knew that rich dude was weaseling his way into this family. I never should have agreed for you all to go on that trip."

Glaring contemptuously at Ashley, he emphasized each word with another slam on the coffee table. "I...just...*knew* it!"

The dogs barked louder, running around the room between them.

He rocked to his feet and shook his finger in her face, eyes shooting sparks. "You've been acting weird ever since you came home from that trip, avoiding me, not wanting to share our bed." Distrust colored his voice. "Are you sleeping with him?"

"Of course not!" Ashley stood up to face Noah, her arms crossed in front of her chest. "I can't believe you would ask me that! Our marriage was in trouble long before Steve."

"*Aha!*" Noah barked out a mean laugh. "So you admit Steve is part of you wanting to break up."

"Settle down. I was really hoping we could have a calm mature discussion." She sat back down in her recliner and motioned for Noah to sit down as well. "Please lower your voice. You're upsetting the dogs."

Noah sat grudgingly and motioned toward her. "Talk."

On the edge of breaking down, she drew in a quivering breath and prayed for the right words. Her eyes filled with tears. "Noah, I *love* you and always will. But our family cannot continue on this same pattern with your work being top priority. Our life has become nothing but a series of tasks without joy or peace." Her eyes connected with Noah's, not turning away from his angry glare. "The romance and companionship are gone. Between work, home, and the girls, I'm running ragged. The thing that hurts the most is that you don't seem to notice or care. All you think about is your work!"

She twisted her wedding ring. "Yes, I'll be honest. Being with Steve stirred up some feelings, but I promise you I did not act on them. I would *never* cheat on you."

Noah's face reddened with fury. "You already *are* cheating on me, even if it's just in your mind!"

His words hit home. A guilty flush bloomed on her cheeks. "I understand your job is demanding, dangerous, and important." She straightened her spine, voice strengthening. "However, my job is important too. I was deeply hurt when you forgot the promises you made to me and the girls."

Noah held up his hand to cut into her discussion.

"I'm talking. You'll get your chance when I'm finished, okay? Let's be respectful."

He nodded and placed both hands firmly on his knees.

Ashley continued, "If our marriage is going to be healed, we *both* need to work on things and make some changes." She looked up at Noah. "Are you willing to do that?"

"Is it my turn to talk now? Or is this all about you and your feelings?" he spat.

Ashley waved him on to continue and sat back in the chair, listening. This was *so* hard. But the walls had to be broken down before they could be rebuilt.

"In all fairness, you understood when we met that you were signing up for a relationship with a firefighter. It's my calling...my duty." He raked his fingers through his short hair. "It's not like I'm playing golf with the boys or out fishing. I'm risking my life and the life of my crew *every...single...day.*" He gazed into her eyes resolutely. "Look. I'll admit fire season has gotten out of hand with the changing climate." He threw his hands up. "But I have no control over it. Don't you think I would rather be home than fighting fire for weeks on end? People are losing their lives, homes, and properties. I've lost firefighters and dozer operators." He let out a frustrated growl. "*Everyone* is suffering, Ashley. Not just *you.* Not just the *girls.*"

"Don't turn this on me, Noah. It's not that you're a firefighter. Emma, Katie, and I are so proud of you and respect and appreciate all you and the crew do to keep people safe. The key issue is that work has become this monstrous beast...out of control. I think the problem is you don't know how to compartmentalize it." She grasped his hands in hers, tears spilling over. She wiped them away with a dash of her fingers. "I think the best thing to do is find a good Christian counselor, someone who can objectively help us with our issues. Meanwhile, I would like you to move out of the house and allow us to have some thinking and processing space."

Noah tossed her hands away from his. "I don't get it. You complain that I'm never here, and now you want me to move out? That makes no sense. Unless you want the coast clear for your boyfriend to move in. Is that it?" He smacked his hand on his leg. "Wow, Ashley! You talk the Christian talk, but you sure aren't living it. Are you?" He stood and walked to the door, turning briefly with a heartbreaking glance in her direction.

"You're making a lot of assumptions which are absolutely not true." Ashley took a deep breath and let it out slowly. "Wait, I have something more to say."

He turned back to face her. "What? More good news?"

"I wanted to share with you that I had a long talk with my supervisor yesterday. They're short-staffed during the Thanksgiving holiday for both the NICU and transport team. She also told me I was in danger of being taken off the transport team if I don't pull more shifts." She gave him a pleading look. "This is as important to me as your firefighting is to you, and it's also my career. I told her I would work as many shifts and transport team rotations as she needed. I spoke with your mom yesterday, and she's willing to keep the girls over the holiday in the event you get called out. Right now, the plan is I'll take them to your parents' house on Wednesday afternoon. They have a minimum day. I can pick them up Sunday afternoon or you can bring them home."

Noah shook his head. "If that's what you want."

"It's what I have to do if I want to stay on the transport team. I have duties and responsibilities to my career as well."

Noah trudged down the hallway, shoulders slumped. He turned back once more. "Do the girls or my family know what's going on? Or am I the only one being blindsided?"

"The girls know we're having relationship difficulties. I haven't discussed anything with your parents," Ashley said in a quiet voice. "I felt that was your decision to make."

Noah continued down the hallway toward their bedroom.

"Where are you going?" Ashley called out.

"To pack my bags and get out of your way."

"Where will you stay?"

"I'll be at the firehouse until I figure something out."

Ashley sank into the recliner, hands over her eyes, tears streaming down her face. Tears over what they used to be and what they had become. How could they ever bridge the gap which was daily becoming wider? A desperate part of her wanted to run after him and scream. *Don't leave. Let's work this out.* While part of her believed they needed this separation. And this wasn't even the hard part. Now she had to break the news to the girls.

20

As expected, the girls reacted strongly to the news of their parents' separation with tears, anger, and storming off to their rooms. Ashley felt like the worst mom ever. And the worst wife. *How could I do this to our family?* All she had wanted since her childhood was to be a good mom, wife, and nurse. *Now I'm a failure at all three.*

The long night dragged slowly by. She checked the messages on her cell phone for the hundredth time. None from Noah. Ashley had never seen him so angry and hurt. *But yet...he didn't seem to understand where I was coming from and how his work affects our family.* Punching her pillow, she tried to find a comfortable position but instead found herself tossing and turning all night.

*****

At the fire station, Noah was spending a lonely night questioning himself and his relationship with Ashley and with the girls. He had surprised his teammates showing up on his day off, duffel bag over his shoulder.

"What's up, Chief?" his captain motioned him into his private office.

Noah closed the door and quietly shared, "Ashley and I are going through a rough patch, and I need to bunk here for a little while until we can get things straightened out...*if* we can." He ran his hands over his face and blew out a breath. "Doug, I'm trying to do my best. This fire season is out of control. What am I supposed to do?" He threw up his hands, frustration mounting. "It seems like, in her eyes, I can't do anything right."

Doug put a reassuring hand on Noah's shoulder. "A lot of us are going through a hard time with our families and all the time away from them. Hang in there. You guys have a special relationship. I know you can work it out." He gave Noah's shoulder a brotherly pat as he turned to leave the room. "Keep me posted if there's anything I can do, okay?"

"Thanks, man."

*****

"Katie, it's your turn to feed the dogs. I fed them the past three days." Emma stomped down the hall, glaring at Katie.

"*I* fed the cat and changed the litter box, and *I* fed the fish." Katie gave her sister a shove as they passed in the hallway.

Emma shoved back angrily.

Katie shrieked. "Mom! Emma's hitting me."

"Both of you, stop it now!" Ashley shouted. "Dad will be here in ten minutes to pick you up. Bring your bags to the front door, and make sure you packed all your toiletries: toothbrush, hairbrush, and face wash, whatever you might need. Also, pack plenty of clean clothes, including underwear. I don't want to put extra work on Grandma to do laundry *and* cook Thanksgiving dinner for every-one." Walking down the hallway, she called up the stairs, "Get your things together, and then come downstairs. I want to talk with both of you."

She collapsed on a recliner in the living room and gathered her thoughts.

The girls ran down the stairs with Nikki and Callie bounding behind them. They placed their bags by the front door and sulked into the living room. "What's up, Mom?"

She motioned for them to sit. "First off, let's go through the checklist to make sure you've got everything: dog leashes, dog food, feeding bowls, brushes?"

As she itemized the, list Katie and Emma made little check marks in the air with their index fingers.

Ashley smiled. "Okay, guys. Remember, I'm scheduled to work quite a few shifts, including transport shifts, so I plan on staying the weekend at the hospital on-call room."

She had asked the preteen next-door neighbor, Beth, to check in and feed Trina, the hamsters, and the fish daily. She was also going to pick up the mail and newspaper.

"It might be hard to reach me, but Dad will be with you. Speaking of Dad, I haven't mentioned our separation to his family."

The girls' faces darkened.

Ashley held up her hand. "Let me finish. Dad will decide when he wants to discuss our situation with his parents. Please keep this within our family for now. Our marriage troubles don't need to be the Thanksgiving topic of conversation. Everyone just thinks I need to work, which I do."

"Okay," they sullenly replied.

Emma's eyes glittered with tears. "It's so unfair!" Tears ran down her cheeks. "Why can't we be a happy family like we used to?"

Katie wiped tears from her face as well. "Yeah. I don't like living apart from Dad. I want us to be together again."

Seeing her daughters' sad faces tugged at her heartstrings. "Dad and I are going to start counseling after the holidays. Maybe we can work things out. No promises, but we'll try. Okay?"

She swept both of her girls into a hug and kissed the tops of their heads. "Always remember I love you."

*****

The Thanksgiving holiday weekend was busy as expected. The NICU was short-staffed compounded by a constant flurry of activity with multiple transports from outlying hospitals. Ashley's twelve-hour shifts turned into sixteen-plus-hour shifts to keep up with the demand, but she didn't mind working more hours. She had no other responsibilities outside of work, which was kind of freeing for a change.

Her supervisor, Michelle, approached her in the hallway. "Thank you so much. You've been such a great help. I appreciate you giving up your holiday." She motioned for Ashley to follow her into the supply room. "How are you holding up? The girls okay?"

Ashley gave a little smile. "Thanks for asking. It's been rough for everyone. I'm checking into marriage counseling once we're past the holidays." She shrugged. "Still hoping we can work this out."

Michelle smiled warmly. "Of course. Please let me know if I can be of any help. Have you given any more thought to the master's degree proposal we discussed?"

Ashley pushed her bangs out of her eyes. "I've thought about it a lot, and I love the idea and challenge, but life has been so mixed up and crazy I haven't been able to process it. Can I get back to you after the holidays?"

"Absolutely." Michelle patted her on the back. "Hang in there."

Stepping back out into the main NICU area, Ashley heard a familiar voice calling her name.

"Hey, Ash!" Laurie smiled and waved.

She grinned back. "Hey! I didn't know you were working today."

"They netted me with the words double time. It pays the bills. Especially with preteen boys and a teen daughter who think they need every new video game and designer this or that. It's totally out of control."

Ashley laughed at her friend's dramatic expression.

"I'm thankful Katie is happy with her Breyer horses and the weekly horseback riding lesson. Emma loves her dance classes, but I've got a feeling both of those are going to get more expensive as time goes on. Katie is already talking about owning a horse, and Emma will be driving in a few years." Ashley groaned.

Laurie pulled her aside into the linen room. "Lots of talk around the fire station about you and Noah separating, just so you're aware."

"Who's talking? What are they saying?" Ashley probed.

Laurie waved her hand breezily. "Oh, you know how people are, anything new to break up the ordinary. That new firefighter, Kat, was surprised. She thought you guys had the perfect marriage."

"Is she that girl with the long red hair? I saw her at the Red Light ball last summer."

"Yeah, she's gorgeous."

Drop-dead gorgeous. "Well, things aren't always what you think they are."

"Funny, that's what Kat said too. She said most women who had a man like Noah would never have cut him loose to be fair game."

"She said that? He's not fair game or on the market. We just need some space to work things out." Ashley felt her blood pressure rising. Her fists clenched by her side.

"Just remember you have someone waiting in the wings too." Laurie arched an eyebrow at her. "Look, people talk. It doesn't mean anything. I've got to get back to my section. There are micro preemie twenty-four-week twins due to arrive shortly. It's going to be busy, and I agreed to pull a sixteen-hour shift. Going to earn that double time the hard way, I guess."

She grinned. "Don't forget about David and my holiday party next Friday. It's going to be fun. Just so you're aware, Noah's invited too." Waving, she hustled into her section to receive the incoming transports.

Still angry, Ashley walked up and down the hallway taking deep breaths before returning to the NICU.

21

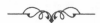

Ashley finished her report to the oncoming night shift and turned her thoughts toward home. Her Thanksgiving week work commitment was completed, and she was looking forward to seeing the girls, their pets, and all the comforts of home. She missed Noah too.

As she drove, her thoughts spun with visions of her husband with another woman, and one far younger. *Stop it! Remember,* you *were the one who asked* him *to leave.* A sinister little voice in her head whispered, *But* you *wanted to be the one who had someone waiting. You wanted to be the one in control.* The voice kept swirling jealous thoughts as Ashley tensed her grip on the wheel. It jeered in her ear. *People always leave you, don't they? You know why? Because you are unlovable. Even your parents couldn't stand to be around you.*

A dark wave of depression overwhelmed her as she pulled into the garage, seeing the house lights shining. She swept into the kitchen and plastered a smile on her face. "Hello. I'm home."

A cacophony of barking dogs and excited screams of "Mom!" filled the air.

Trina sashayed her furry tail against her calves, meowing loudly.

"I want to hear all about your week at Grandma's and Grandpa's, but first, let me change out of these germ-infested scrubs, okay? I'll be right back."

Walking though the living room, she paused in front of Noah sitting in his recliner. A bubble of happiness swiftly rose inside her at the sight of her family together under one roof.

She smiled warmly. "Hi. I missed all of you. How's your family?"

"Everyone is fine," he said curtly, giving her a look she couldn't interpret. "Well, I'll be on my way." He stood and called out, "Bye, girls. Love you."

Katie and Emma came running into the living room.

"Please don't go, Dad," Katie implored.

Emma chimed in, "We want you here. Home. With us." She sniffed and wiped tears from her eyes. "Together as a family. Like we used to be."

Noah shot a glare at Ashley. "But that's not what your mother wants." He stomped to the door and let himself out without another glance.

Ashley's throat clamped with emotion, and her heart fell as Noah walked out of their home and the life they had built together.

"It's all your fault, Mom! I hate my life!" Emma blurted out.

Katie nodded. Crying, they ran upstairs to their rooms. The gloom of depression closed in silent and swift. Ashley trudged down the hallway into the bedroom to change.

*****

The following Friday night, Ashley took a parting glance in the full-length mirror. She was wearing a gold-threaded knee-length cocktail dress with a butterfly hemline that swirled when she walked. She brushed a layer of golden bronzer followed by blush on her drawn pale cheeks. A swipe of rose-pink lipstick and gloss finished her makeup. *Hmm…my clothes are looser, but my face looks blotchy, pinched, and tired.* The stress of the separation, the girls, and responsibilities at home was taking its toll.

The girls were having a sleepover at Jackie and Nick's so Ashley could attend Laurie and David's party. She had tried to graciously excuse herself from attending, but Laurie wouldn't hear it. Ashley was dreading seeing their friends' reactions to the separation. She knew from seeing other couples separate that people always picked sides. Her emotional state was too raw and bruised to cope with what other people thought.

She gave herself one last glance in the mirror, slipped her arms into her winter coat, and turned for the door. Determined to at least be social, especially on behalf of her friend Laurie, who had worked so hard putting this party together, she swept aside her thoughts. Tuning the car radio to Christmas music, she hummed along as she drove.

*****

It was a chilly, foggy early December night as her car pulled up in front of Laurie and David's festive home. Unfastening her seat belt, Ashley grabbed her clutch and hostess gift of a fine champagne. She shivered in the frosty evening air and pulled her coat tighter. From the laughter and jolly Christmas carols emanating from the house, she could see the party was in full swing. *Boy, the Jones family sure love a party.*

Pasting on what she hoped looked like a fun holiday smile, she rapped on the door. *I wonder if Noah is here.* Excited at the prospect of seeing him, but worried it could be awkward, she chewed her bottom lip.

David flung open the door and drew her into a big bear hug. "Welcome, Ashley! So glad to see you."

She squeezed him back just as tightly and handed him the gift. "Merry Christmas. This is to help make the season brighter."

"Thanks." He glanced at the label appreciatively. "Um. Good stuff. Let's open it up. Come on in." Ashley started to remove her coat as she scanned the crowded room. Boisterous laughter filled the air. When she turned her head toward the shrieks, there was Noah. He was sitting in a chair with his arms securely fitted around Kat, a huge ear-to-ear grin on his face.

Kat had a wine glass in her hand as she snuggled her body against his. She was wearing a skintight gold lamé bodysuit that left nothing to the imagination and red high heels that matched her lips. Noah looked like he was having the time of his life. People gathered around, toasting and laughing.

Ashley froze in disbelief, one arm out of her coat and the other still in. People pressed all around her, calling out greetings, seemingly oblivious to the drama playing out in front of them. The party sounds became high and tinny as the blood drained from her face.

Feeling dizzy and sick, she took a breath and turned away. She snaked through the partying crowd toward the door without looking back.

Choking back tears, she hurried to her car and slammed the door. As she drove off, she saw Laurie run out behind her, frantically waving, trying to stop her from leaving. Crushed, she didn't even slow down. All she knew was Noah's arms were around the young, gorgeous Kat. He had already moved on.

A breathtaking sob burst out of her chest followed by a rain of heavy tears. Her vision blinded by the sheen of tears, she pulled over on the side of the road and dropped her head down onto the steering wheel. *How could he have his arms around someone else already?* And right in front of their friends, people laughing, not a care in the world like they didn't even notice that her world had fallen apart.

Ashley didn't see the police cruiser pulling up behind her until the officer was tapping on her window with his flashlight. Startled, she sat upright and wiped her eyes. The officer swept his flashlight around the interior of the car as she rolled down the window.

He focused on her tearful face and streaking mascara. "Everything okay, Miss? You've been drinking?"

She shook her head, choking back a sob. "No, Officer. I received some bad news. That's all. I pulled off the road to pull myself together before driving home."

Quickly assessing the scene, the officer checked her license and registration. "Okay, Ms. Smith. You can proceed home. Please be careful, the fog is getting bad. Keep your low beams on."

With a wave of her hand, Ashley pulled back out onto the road to the privacy of home.

*****

Ashley was a mess. She couldn't eat, barely slept, and could only garner enough energy to perform the necessary tasks. Every time she closed her eyes, all she could see was Kat's ruby red lips and Noah's grinning face over and over. She hadn't seen or spoken with Noah since the party a week ago. Three times a week, he would pick up the girls from school and then drop them off the next morning. He had rented an apartment nearby, so the girls stayed overnight.

Subtly questioning the girls produced no information.

"How's Dad?" she had asked that morning over breakfast.

"Fine," came their stony reply.

She tried to keep her prying casual. "Oh, what did you do? Does he have any new friends?"

Emma sighed. "We did homework, had dinner, and then went to bed. We haven't met any new friends."

"Does Dad seem happy? Or happier?"

Emma scanned her mother with a scathing eye. "He seems happier than *you*. Enough questions."

The girls stomped off to their rooms to pick fights with each other over inconsequential things.

She raked her greasy hair from her forehead, gathered it into a knot, and twisted a rubber band she had removed from her wrist to make a messy bun. She looked down at her stained baggy sweats and sighed aloud to the empty room. Heartbroken, Ashley grieved the loss of their once-happy family as she shuffled off to do the laundry.

*****

Steve called Ashley almost daily after she dropped off the girls at school and was driving to work. Right on time, the incoming call from Steve lit up. Hesitantly, she pressed the speaker to answer. "Hi, beautiful. How's your day going so far? Have you filed for divorce yet? Can I come up and see you when Noah has the girls? I can fly up and get you. We can go to San Francisco for the weekend. I miss you so much."

Oddly, Ashley didn't have the same desire to spend time alone with Steve. Her head just felt so jumbled with thoughts of Noah and

Kat and their family. *I pushed him straight into her arms. I'm the one destroying the family with my selfishness. It's all my fault.*

"Steve, I need some time to process everything. Please."

"Okay, sorry if I'm putting too much pressure on you. I'm just so eager to spend time with you. I forget how I felt after my divorce. It takes time, and I'm willing to give that to you"—he paused—"because I love you."

But I don't think I love you.

Ashley drew back from the phone, covering her mouth in shamefaced remorse. She had not only hurt her family but Steve too. She was mortified at the snowball effect of her actions.

Taking a shuddering breath, she realized the truth hiding in her troubled heart. *I love Noah and what we used to have.* Nausea cramped her stomach and crept up her throat. "I'll see you in two days when you drop off the girls. Noon at the private airport, right?"

"Yes, can't wait to see you. The girls are beside themselves to see their northern sisters."

"Katie and Emma planned all kinds of fun things. I've got the next week off to run them around. See you soon. Bye." Ashley turned into a parking spot in the hospital garage, hung up the phone, and cradled her head in her hands. What had she done?

Greeting her at the staff entrance, Rodney took in her sad demeanor. "Everything okay, Ashley?"

"Oh, you know, sometimes life can be a little challenging."

"Well, you be sure to contact security when your shift ends, and one of us will walk you to your car. More and more stuff happening, and I want you all to be safe."

Turning, she gave him a watery smile. "Thank you for watching over us, Rodney. We appreciate you."

"We appreciate all of you nurses, doctors, and all the first responders for everything you do," he replied earnestly. "I hope your day goes better. Hang in there."

She waved with the tips of her fingers and entered the door.

22

Driving to the airport two days later, Ashley chuckled at her daughters' ecstatic expressions. The car buzzed with their excited voices discussing all their fun plans. The jet swooped in and landed smoothly. Ashley pressed her hands down her wool shirt. It was chilly and frosty, so she had dressed warmly with a leather bomber jacket, woolen scarf, and knee-high boots. The girls were jumping up and down as the door opened and the ladder slid down.

"Hi! Hi!" Cara and Lexie skipped down the steps into Katie's and Emma's waiting arms.

"We are going to have *so* much fun!" they squealed.

Steve rushed down the steps to envelop Ashley in his arms. "You look fantastic!"

Emma and Katie turned to stare at their mom with a perplexed expression.

Returning the hug, she whispered a warning, "Watching eyes." Ashley tried to cover up the awkward moment with a laugh. She threw up her hands in an airy gesture. "No worries. It's exciting stuff seeing the northern and southern sisters together." She turned to the girls. "We're so glad you're here. We have lots of fun things planned."

"Thank you, Mrs. Smith," they said politely.

"You can call me Ashley, okay?" Taking a second glance at Steve's girls, she noticed they both had plastered on makeup. Cara especially was wearing heavy eye makeup and lipstick. *Hmm, I didn't notice that last fall. Looks like someone is growing up or trying to* look *grown up.*

Steve gave his daughters one last hug and a playful wag of his index finger. "Be on your best behavior."

He turned back to Ashley, glancing over to see if the girls were watching. They were in animated conversation discussing their planned adventures.

He took her hands in his and placed a gentle kiss on her forehead. "Thank you for taking care of the girls. I look forward to returning the favor." His bright blue eyes looked adoringly into hers.

Ashley withdrew her hands and stepped back. "Have a good conference. We'll see you in a week. Safe flight."

Steve bounded up the stairs into the jet. He blew a kiss as he pulled up the ladder and secured the airplane's door.

As he taxied down the runway, Ashley and the girls buckled in. "Who's hungry?" she called out.

"We are! We are!"

Adjusting her shoulder harness, she put the car into gear. "Well, let's get this party started."

"Yeah!" came a resounding cheer from the back seats.

*****

If Ashley had been exhausted before Cara and Lexi arrived, she was even more so now. Keeping up with four preteens on top of all her personal drama was almost too much. For the most part, the girls seemed to be having a blast, but there were also some strange undercurrents.

There had been a lot of whispered secrets, unhappy expressions, and slamming of doors. It made her uneasy that some outfits Cara and Lexie wore were more provocative than was appropriate for preteens. The four of them did not hang out together as they had before. It was definitely two separate sets of friends. Ashley didn't like that. Her girls had always been close.

She had also picked up some weird vibes from both Emma and Katie that were disconcerting. It was as if they were hiding secrets. Steve was returning that afternoon to pick up Cara and Lexie. Afterward, they were going to have a frank talk about what was going on.

After the girls were picked up and safely on their way home, Ashley rounded up Emma and Katie for a chat. They all sat down in the living room.

"Let's talk, girls. How did the week go for you?"

Uneasy glances passed between Emma and Katie.

"Well," Emma stammered, "it was fun to see them, and we appreciate everything you did. You went out of your way, and we know this is a hard time for you."

Katie waved her hand at her sister. "Emma, tell her."

Emma pursed her lips and drew in a breath. "I don't want to be a tattletale, but there are some things you should probably know."

Ashley's antenna perked up. "What is it, Emma? Please tell me."

Emma picked at her cuticle. "Well, remember when we went to the mall?"

Ashley nodded.

Emma hesitantly continued. "Well, as soon as you were out of sight, Cara took off her jacket and was wearing this skintight top. It was a belly shirt too. She also clipped on a fake nose ring and belly button ring, and she was strutting around this group of boys."

Katie piped in, "And she had a pack of cigarettes. Emma, tell Mom about the other thing too."

Emma focused on her cuticles again.

Ashley leaned in and smiled encouragingly. "Please tell me, Emma. You can trust me."

Her face twisted with shock as her daughter continued, "She sent texts to the boys we met at the mall. Pictures of her posing...in her underwear." Fat tears rolled down Emma's cheeks.

Ashley cringed. Emma swallowed, her jaw quavering. "Cara was trying to arrange for us to hook-up at the bowling alley. She wanted me to lie to you. She also wanted us to sneak out of the house at night and have these boys pick us up to go to a party."

Ashley drew back in horror. All this was going on under her roof! She felt terrible for allowing this to happen. She had sensed something was off but had no idea it was any of this! "The boys are a lot older than us Mom. I didn't like it, so I told her no. Cara said I was a baby and needed to grow up."

Ashley gasped. She knew there was something suspicious, but this? She grabbed a couch pillow and held it to her middle to ground herself and be composed so the girls would feel free to talk.

Taking a calming breath, she tried to hide her emotions. "Thank you for telling me, Emma. I'm proud of you for staying strong and doing the right thing. I know that must have been hard for you."

Emma lamented, "Cara was not the same girl we had so much fun with during fall break. I don't want to be around her anymore."

"Does her dad know what's going on?"

She shook her head. "I don't think so. He's not around that much. Cara and Lexi mostly live with their mom. It sounded like she lets them do whatever they want. They even had their own credit card with no limit!"

Emma swiped tears from her eyes. "She didn't want to do any of the stuff we had planned. It was all about makeup, clothes, and meeting boys."

Katie chimed in, "Lexi had changed too. She wore makeup and didn't want to play with my Breyer horses. She told me her dad was rich, and he would buy her a real horse, not some stupid toy horse."

Ashley sat back on the couch and clenched the pillow.

Emma's dark chocolate eyes, *just like Noah's*, rose to meet hers. "Cara had marijuana."

"Oh, no," Ashley replied in a weak voice.

"I told her I don't do drugs. I also told her I would tell you if she did drugs in our house."

"Good for you, Emma. I'm proud of you for standing up to her. That takes a lot of courage."

Ashley's world crumpled as she heard Emma's next words. "She did talk about you and Steve. She said the two of you are going to get married once your divorce is final." Her voice trembled. "Is that true?"

Katie jumped in with an imploring gaze. "Mom, is it?"

23

Adrenaline shot through Ashley's veins. She felt dizzy and out of body. Taking a deep breath, she contemplated her daughters' apprehensive faces. Knowing she was the cause was almost more than she could bear. Her world was spinning out of control. Noah had moved out of the house and was with someone else. Steve and his daughters were not the people she thought they were. What a mess she had made of things—all because she wasn't able to cope with her husband being on fires, saving lives and property?

The dark heckling voice returned. *You're a horrible self-centered person. Look at them and what you've done! It's all* your *fault.* Shame and guilt made her pulse beat faster. The voice became louder and darker. *You never should've invited Steve over for dinner. You brought all this chaos into your home and family.* Your *fault.* Your *fault.*

Struggling with the oppressiveness of her thoughts, she said a silent, fierce prayer. *Get behind me, evil one in the name of Jesus.* Immediately, she felt a sense of resolve. She got up and walked over and bent down in front of the girls. Putting one arm around each of them, she held them tight. Tears streamed down her face. "I'm *so sorry* for what you're going through. Please forgive me." At that moment, her mind was firmly made up.

"No, I am *not* marrying Steve, and it is my hope that Dad and I *will not* divorce." Her voice broke. "We still have some things to work through, but I want you to know, I am committed to keeping our family together, and most of all, I love you. I love you for who you are and your strength of character."

They formed a tight circle, bound by love. Ashley pledged to do whatever it took to make things right with Noah and the girls.

She looked upward to God. *Thank you, Father, for watching over my daughters. Please help our family. Heal us with your love.*

*****

After the girls went to bed, Ashley spent hours in front of the fireplace praying. She heard the Lord speaking to her as clearly as if he were standing beside her. *Don't go back down the same path—move forward on a new path. One I have chosen for you.*

Scanning the Bible, she was drawn to the words of Galatians 2:20. *I have been crucified with Christ, and I no longer live, but Christ lives in me.*

Ashley prayed God would crucify her old ways and patterns that were destroying her family. She knew in her heart she had not been faithful to Noah. She prayed for forgiveness. They had taken a vow before God and man fifteen years ago that *"two shall become one."* She prayed the Lord would renew their love, reignite their marriage, and give them redeeming love and forgiveness to restore their commitment.

Emotionally and physically spent, she crawled under the covers and pulled the cozy blankets over her shoulders. She glanced at the empty side of the bed. A renewed strength to fight hard for her marriage emerged. She would go to war if needed. Resolved, she turned over and fell into a peaceful deep slumber.

Her alarm went off at six the next morning. She felt more rested and refreshed than she had for months. *Thank you, Lord.* She had needed her batteries recharged to do what she needed to do.

She sipped a cup of coffee while the girls slept, steeling herself for the first item on the agenda. Talk to Steve. This was not going to be pleasant. She found his name in her contacts list and punched the video chat button.

He picked up on the second ring. "Morning, sunshine! I was just thinking of you." His voice lowered huskily as he gave her a seductive smile. "I had the sweetest dream of us last night. I woke up wishing you were next to me."

Swallowing dryly, Ashley reached for her water glass. "Do you have a few minutes, Steve?"

"Of course. I always have time for you, my love."

"Well," Ashley hesitated, taking a sip of her water, "I don't think you're going to like what I need to tell you."

"That doesn't sound good." He moved off-screen, and she heard his office door close in the background before he returned with a look of concern. "What's up?"

Ashley proceeded to share with him what Emma and Katie had told her. "Steve, I'm not only dismayed at what transpired, but I'm concerned about the choices the girls are making, particularly Cara. She could end up in a bad life-changing situation."

Steve was quiet for a long moment, then let out a long exhale. "Wow. I had noticed the makeup was a bit extreme, but I just thought this was something all adolescent girls went through. The girls were so excited about seeing their northern sisters. I had no idea this kind of stuff was going on. I'll talk with Stephanie, and we'll both decide how best to handle this."

Steve paced around his office. Ashley could see him picking up a picture of Cara and Lexie, smiling at their young carefree faces. Then his face stiffened, and he frowned. "Thanks for telling me. I'm sure it was very difficult for you and the girls. I'm so sorry about their behavior." He set down the picture, strode across the room, then stared out the window into the bay for several moments.

His boyish grin returned as he refocused on her face. "Hey, speaking of the girls, have you and Noah discussed custody? My girls stay with me every other weekend and two weeks a year. We share holidays. Maybe you should make the same arrangement so we can travel together." Seeming to forget the seriousness of the previous conversation, his voice rose in excitement. "I sure wish you were here right now. It's a beautiful day. We could be sailing in the bay."

Ashley clenched her fists, drawing on her inner strength. "Steve, I've decided to try to work things out with Noah. I'm sorry if I've led you to believe we could have a relationship, but this is my final decision. Our family needs to be together. The girls and I had a wonderful time with you last fall, and I appreciate all you did. I truly never meant to hurt you."

"But, Ashley, please. I know we could share a beautiful life together. At least let me try."

She twisted a tissue in her fingers. "I wish you and the girls the best. Just so you're aware, the main reason I'm breaking it off with you is because I still love Noah. I want more than anything for our family to be together. Please try to understand."

His grin faded. "But what if Noah doesn't want to get back together with you? What then? Would that change your mind?"

Ashley considered his words carefully. "No, it wouldn't. I've spent a lot of time in prayer. It has become clear I don't believe that it's God's will for us to be together. He has a different plan for you and for me. You're a wonderful man, and I wish you the best. Take care. I have to go." She hung up the phone and reached for a tissue.

Ashley took a few minutes to settle her racing heart and explore her thoughts about ending her relationship with Steve. She evaluated her motives in allowing him back into her life and realized they were not based on her Christian values but on vanity, ego, and a lack of self-control. "Lord, please forgive me for my self-centered actions. Forgive me for hurting my family. I pray if it's your will that you'll heal our marriage and family. Help me to follow your will and your purpose. Amen."

She pressed Noah's number and held her breath as it rang. He answered. "What?"

Ashley sat back in her chair, reeling from the hostile tone in his voice. *Have we really drifted so far that we can't even be civil?* Then another disturbing thought popped into her head. *Maybe he's not alone.* The image of Kat snuggled in Noah's lap, both of them smiling and laughing, flashed into her brain. Her throat became dry and parched as she attempted to squeak out the reason for her call.

"Ashley? Are you there? What do you want? I'm busy."

Blood rushed into her face as she recalled Kat's red lips and skin-tight gold lamé jumpsuit. The way Noah looked at her with desire. *They* are *together! I knew it. And I'm interrupting something.* Images of what that *something* could be spun in her imagination.

This was it. Their marriage was over. There was no going back or patching things up. He no longer loved her or wanted to be with her. From the angry tone of his voice, he sounded like he hated her and wanted her out of his life. He had moved on and was with someone else, someone younger and more desirable. Her heart shattered.

"I'm sorry. I misdialed," she said in a small voice.

Disconnecting the call, she put her hands to her face.

*****

Punching the end call button, Noah shook his head at the phone. There was something weird about the call, but he couldn't put his finger on what it was. His phone rang again. He felt badly about the way he had answered the phone. He was just so frustrated and missed Ashley and their family. Now he was about to be deployed to another fire and wouldn't be around to patch things up.

Thinking it might be her calling him back, he snatched the phone without looking at the caller ID. "Hello?"

"Chief Smith, this is Rick from the Command Center. Team Four activated. Your orders are to assemble at the San Diego Country Fairground by midnight tonight for the transition briefing." After a pause he continued, "They have several new fires that are fast moving and have already lost several homes."

He was on call for Command Team Four, and things were heating up again in Southern California despite it being early December. He brushed his hand through his short hair. *This is crazy, definitely the worst fire season I've ever seen.* His broad steps ate up the room as he grabbed his go bag, hustled out of the apartment, and jumped into his fire vehicle.

Shaking off Ashley's strange phone call, he set his mind on the task ahead. He maneuvered his fire vehicle out of the parking lot and settled in for the long drive and thought of another sleepless, prolonged siege.

*****

Hearing the girls pound down the stairs, followed by Nikki and Callie, Ashley brushed the tears off her cheeks and plastered on a smile. "Morning, girls. How about French toast for breakfast?"

Katie and Emma pumped enthusiastic fists in the air.

"Scrambled eggs too?" Katie asked.

Ashley smiled. "You bet."

The girls swirled around her, feeding the animals and setting the table. Sounds of happy laughter filled the air as they chatted about their morning plans. Ashley knew in her heart that she had made the right decision breaking things off with Steve. There was sadness, too, now that she had neither Noah nor Steve. She was alone.

Watching the girls, her heart filled with love. *No. I am not alone ever! I have God and two amazing daughters. That's enough. More than enough.*

A quiet peacefulness filled her soul, and she heard a whisper, "*Be still and know that I am God.*"

Later in the evening, Ashley noticed a voice mail from Noah on her phone. "Hi, Ashley. I apologize for being short with you on the phone earlier today. Wanted to tell you Command Team Four has been activated. I'm driving to San Diego. You know the drill. I don't know how long I'll be gone."

A long pause ensued. "I probably won't be back to take my turn caring for the girls. Just wanted to give you a heads up. Sorry, but it's out of my control. I'll call when I have more information. Bye."

Ashley ended the voice mail message with a sad grimace. There was no "I love you" or "Miss you," but for once, she wasn't angry Noah would be gone and she would have to pick up the slack. Instead, she found she missed him, loved him, and prayed for God to protect him and bring him and the strike team home safely.

She vowed to fight for him, for them, their family. "Please, Lord, work a miracle in our marriage."

Sleep was elusive. She flipped the pillow to the cool side and burrowed under the covers. Thoughts of starting life over again without Noah by her side brought back the deep emptiness of her childhood.

24

If she was going to have *any* hope of making things work with Noah, Ashley was going to have to work through some strongholds from her past. On the advice of a trusted mentor at church, she made an appointment with a Christian counselor. She had hoped to attend marriage counseling with Noah, but fire season and his anger toward her made that unrealistic for now. At least she could go forward with finding some help for herself.

As she walked into the office, the counselor, Beth, rose to meet her at the door. She shook Ashley's hand. "It's so good to meet you, Ashley. Please, sit wherever you feel comfortable."

Ashley settled into a soft chair next to the window. The room had an inviting and peaceful presence. The office was tastefully decorated with cozy pillows and throws. Beautiful photographs of nature adorned the walls. Gentle instrumental music was playing, and several boxes of tissues were set out all around.

Beth opened the conversation. "So you mentioned on the phone that a friend from your Bible study referred you to me."

Ashley smiled a bit nervously. "Yes, Linda has been a tremendous mentor to me over the years." She swallowed uneasily and continued in a trembling voice. "It's uncomfortable for me to talk about myself, but I'm willing to give it a try." She plucked a tissue from the box, surprised how quickly emotions rose inside her.

Beth smiled reassuringly, placing her hand on Ashley's. "Thank you for taking the first critical step of any healing process, making the call and showing up for the appointment. That takes a lot of courage and determination. Let's start by praying and asking Him to guide and bless our time."

Ashley wiped the tears welling in her eyes as she bowed her head.

Afterward, Beth looked at Ashley with compassion and years of skillful training. "Ready to begin?"

The hour flew by as Ashley shared her story of growing up in a lonely household with absent parents. Feeling unwanted and unlovable. Tigger's death. Her deep-seated fear that she would be abandoned again by her husband and family. Beth listened, nodding along, not interjecting but encouraging her to share her thoughts without judgment.

At the end of the session, Ashley felt drained, but she also felt a new lightness at having shared her deepest thoughts, feelings, and hurts. It was freeing and healing.

Beth grasped Ashley's hands lightly. "Great work, Ashley. I look forward to continuing our sessions and feel God's presence in your situation. I'd like to leave you with one thought to pray about until we meet again." Her warm eyes regarded Ashley's. "No *human* is ever meant to hold in place your worth or fill your soul. Only *God,* his Son, Jesus Christ, and his Holy Spirit can do that."

She smiled encouragingly. "I would like to give you a home-work assignment before our next session, if that's okay.

Ashley leaned forwarded and nodded.

"I would like you to spend thirty minutes every day with the Lord in his word and in prayer."

"I will."

Standing up, Beth smiled. "Great. I'll see you next week."

Stepping out of the office into the chilly December afternoon, Ashley was encouraged that she was on a new path. As she buckled her seat belt, she felt enlightened and revitalized. This new path was not going to be easy to negotiate. Obstacles and roots in the pathway would try to trip her up, but with God, anything was possible.

On her way to pick up the girls from their riding and dance les-sons, she reflected on her session, determined she was going to make the changes she needed to make.

The following counseling sessions continued to help Ashley heal from past hurts and falsehoods she had allowed to fester. She gained new insights into how to let go of who she thought she was and focus instead on who God thought she was and where he was leading her in his divine will and purpose.

Through Beth's gentle guidance, she learned how her emotions led her to develop beliefs which led to actions. Some beliefs and actions she was repeating were not helpful but detrimental to her relationship with Noah. Her disappointment with his forgetting to pick up the girls and keeping his promises was really a matter of needing to forgive and move forward rather than dredging up his shortcomings over and over.

Maybe instead of focusing on how his work takes away from being reliable in helping with the girls, I need to look at what is working and what's not working.

In addition to the counseling sessions with Beth's encouragement, Ashley had joined an online women's study group. It had been many years since she had done anything just for herself outside of the family. She found enjoyment, encouragement, and new friendships. The thick cloud of depression that had loomed over her head for weeks started to lift.

Noah had called a few times, but either she was at work or couldn't answer the phone. The brief messages he left contained the same message; fire siege was in full force, and fire season was far from over.

*****

The winds were fierce, making their efforts to contain the fire futile. As Operations Section Chief, Noah had the impossible task of utilizing the slim available resources where they proved most effective. Fires continued to rage, resources overextended. There just weren't enough boots on the ground nor air attack forces to battle the numerous blazes. The firefight shifted from putting out the fire toward utilizing their limited resources to save lives and property.

Noah clasped his hands behind his neck. He had just been notified that all air tankers and helicopters had been grounded because of the strong erratic winds. He twisted the stiff, taut muscles in his back and neck from side to side, strained from eight hours of driving followed by a midnight briefing and all-night planning session. There hadn't been any significant precipitation in the season thus far. Fire fuels were bone dry. This was bad—very bad.

The county sheriff strode over to the incident base, set up in the local high school gym. Noah's attention was focused on the action unfolding on the tactical radios. The sheriff tapped his finger pointedly on his desk and shouted, "You need to get more resources on this fire. We're getting reports of people trapped in their homes and others unable to evacuate."

Turning, Noah regarded him with steely eyes. "Sir," he said calmly, "all available resources are deployed. We're just stripped."

The sheriff's face pulsed with anger. He pointed his index finger at Noah's chest. "You guys are the largest fire department in the world, and you're telling me you can't do better?"

Noah flushed. Trying to keep his mounting frustration in control, he stood face-to-face. "Sir, your county is not the only one burning in the state. Please, let us do our jobs, and you do yours." He paced away, shaking his head angrily.

"Chief Smith!" a voice across the room called out. "Division F is calling you on the Command Frequency."

Noah ran back to his desk and grabbed the portable radio.

The speaker crackled with static. "Operations, Division F. We're experiencing a significant wind shift, and fire is running to the east, toward Southwest Vista Estates." He shouted over the noise of the howling winds in the background. "Additionally, we are looking at heavy spotting on the ridge into this side of the estates."

More crackling static.

Noah leaned forward, straining to hear every word. The thundering erratic winds made it difficult to hear the radio traffic.

Then Division F continued, "Additionally, unless the winds subside, at this rate of spread, the flame front will probably be there in fifteen minutes or less."

"Operations copies. Can your engines access that area?"

Division F replied, "Negative. There's a brush-filled canyon between us and that ridge. Hose lay only."

"Operations copies," Noah crisply replied.

Captain Townsend, the Team Resource Unit Leader, quickly interjected, "Chief, there's a Type One Engine Strike Team still available in staging."

"Great," Noah said. "Get them on the road to the estates now for structure protection." Captain Townsend turned and quickly sped away as Noah added, "And one more thing. Division A is mostly contained. Ask them to free up any excess engines and send them too!"

"Copy, Chief!"

Without skipping a beat, Noah then turned to another member of his staff. "Tell the incident commander what's happening and ask him to expedite local law enforcement to the estates. Also tell him I strongly suggest we change the voluntary evacuation status to mandatory."

"Got it, Chief."

Noah scanned the tense faces of the surrounding Ops Team and waved them over to the tactical map. Taking a quick gulp from his water bottle, he racked his brain, trying to conjure up resources for the disastrous scene unfolding in Division F.

He took another sip to ease his dry throat. "We have more firefighting resources ordered and en route, but until then, we need to reevaluate what additional resources could be freed up to moved there for now."

The Ops Team nodded and scattered to focus on immediate strategies. It was a long, dangerous night. The unpredictable strong winds persisted with frequent gusts of over eighty miles per hour. The fire was spreading erratically with fire brand embers raining down on the subdivision, creating new fires faster than the firefighters could fight them. Law enforcement attempted to control the ebb and flow of desperate evacuations as the firefighters struggled to contain the hundreds of spot fires in the fierce winds.

Walls of flames soon enveloped neighborhoods, consuming homes and properties with a relentless appetite. Entire blocks of homes were being simultaneously ignited, taking with them those who refused to evacuate or didn't have time or the means to leave. The firestorm was unstoppable. A force of nature no foe could fight.

As morning emerged, and the smoke started to clear, the first members of a damage assessment team assessed the destruction in what was once a peaceful, idyllic community. Now, hundreds of homes and properties had been destroyed. Irreplaceable mementos and possessions lay in smoldering ruins. Along with the horrific fire-fighting was the frantic inventory of those who had been evacuated and those still unaccounted. The difficult task of uncovering possible remains loomed before them.

Hospitals were at capacity with the burned and smoke damaged. Streets and roads were blocked by burned cars and trucks. Fire disaster shelters were hastily being established. Churches and other nonprofits were pooling resources to help the community. The winds had died down enough that air attack could continue the fight from the air, providing some relief to the ground crew. However, weather predictions indicated the high winds would return as the day progressed.

Rubbing his whiskered weary face, Noah reached for the coffeepot. He filled his mug with the dark brew and took a tentative sip, grimacing at the bitter dregs. The weight of the responsibility for these lives bore down on his shoulders. He stretched the tension from his neck and strolled into the Command Center for the seven o'clock morning briefing. *Will this nightmare ever end?*

25

With a sigh of pleasure, Ashley leaned back into the massage chair and relaxed, soaking her feet in the Jacuzzi foot bath. The fragrant smell of lavender wafted through the air as her tight back muscles loosened under the kneading motions of the chair. The sessions with Beth brought to light the fact that Ashley had been running on an empty tank for years.

Her long shifts in the NICU, in addition to the hour commute each way, raising their daughters, and managing the household left little to no time for herself. Subconsciously, she had resented it and Noah. She begrudged him being able to go to work and just concentrate on his work, whereas she worked in a very stressful job *and* juggled all the responsibilities of their home and family.

Pushing her back against the massage chair to reach a particularly sore area, she acknowledged that he, too, had a very stressful and dangerous job. She was concerned about his physical and emotional health. There were always dangerous wildfires but nothing like the past five or so years. Previously, he often worked twenty-four or forty-eight hour shifts with barely a call, especially during the winter months. Working on projects around the station, he would come home happy and rested, ready to tackle home improvement projects. Now, climate change and people living in fire hazard zones changed everything.

Life in general hadn't always been this way either. The responsibilities of work and family seemed to slowly mushroom over time. The girls grew older, and their activities grew too. Out of love for them and wanting them to experience the happy childhood she missed, Ashley had become a "parachute mom."

Beth gently guided her to the conclusion that perhaps she didn't need to be *all* things at *all* times to *all* people, especially when it resulted in running herself ragged and being left feeling empty and unappreciated.

"Ashley, I encourage you not to become a victim of your thoughts or emotions but instead to take them to the Lord and ask for clarity."

"I'll try. What I've been doing definitely isn't working."

"Trust Jesus more than your own ability to make everything work out in your favor."

The words rang true to Ashley's heart and psyche. She put Beth's suggestions and advice into action. Her thirty-minute Bible reading and prayer time grew longer as she poured out her heart to God. She became more emotionally stable and less on a teeter totter of emotions. The dark hissing voice in her head vanished. She purchased a stationary bike and got into the habit of going to bed earlier and waking up an hour earlier to get a workout in before her day started. As a result, she felt more rested, toned, and less depressed. Being a nurse, she knew these things, but she had allowed life and responsibilities to override her common sense, and again, thoughts led to actions which led to patterns.

Beth encouraged her to seek the words of Jesus and his promises. "Choose to believe that God is *with* you, *for you*, and *loves* you."

Ashley looked up at her shyly. "Even when people…or *I* think I'm unlovable?"

"Most definitely. Especially then."

She admired her freshly polished bright-pink toenails and glanced at her phone's news feed. Her lips clenched tight as she read of the destruction and casualties from the fire Noah was assigned. *Lord, please be with Noah and the rest of the fire crews. Give them strength and safety. I pray for all the people affected by this fire, for peace, for protection, for restoration.*

She paid for her mani-pedi and walked into the nearby deli to meet Laurie for lunch. Another of Beth's suggestions for self-healing was to set aside time to have fun with her friends and reconnect with enjoyable activities outside of work and care taking. On Saturday, she was signed up for a beginning watercolor class, something she had wanted to do for years.

*****

Laurie was already seated in a corner booth. Ashley hustled over and enveloped her friend in a warm hug.

"I haven't seen you in weeks," Laurie said.

"Too long," Ashley agreed. "How was your trip back to the East Coast?"

"It was great. We got to visit all the family, aunts, uncles, cousins, and grandparents. Weather was amazing, and the maple syrup harvest was just starting." Laurie smiled and motioned toward a beautifully wrapped gift. "I got you a present. Open it!"

Ashley unwrapped the gift to find a perfectly formed maple leaf Christmas ornament brushed with gold. She held it up to the light, twirling it in the air. "I love it. Thank you. I'll find the perfect spot for it on the tree."

She motioned toward the gift she brought for Laurie. "Your turn."

Laurie flashed a smile and peeled back the wrapping. "Oh, it's beautiful! Thank you." She held up the blown glass ornament and examined the tree design inside the globe in blue, purple, and greens.

"It's called the tree of life," Ashley explained. "I found it at a cute little shop on the coast when we visited last summer. When I saw it, I thought of you."

"I love it! So thoughtful. All my favorite colors too." She carefully wrapped the ornament back in its tissue paper and placed it back in the box. "I'll have to find a safe place for this, away from my rowdy boys."

After placing their lunch orders, Ashley and Laurie faced each other across the booth.

"So. Where should we begin?" Laurie took a sip of her water.

Ashley proceeded to tell her about her counseling sessions with Beth and the changes she was making.

"I'm so happy for you. It sounds like you're heading in a good direction." Laurie took a bite of her sandwich, chewed, and delicately wiped her mouth. "Are you going to the wedding this weekend?"

"Wedding? No, who's getting married?"

"Oh, maybe the invitation went to Noah instead." Laurie took a sip from her water glass. "Kat and Josh are getting married on Saturday. You should see them together." Laurie laughed. "They're just adorable and so much in love. It's palpable."

Ashley sputtered her iced tea. "Getting married this Saturday? Kat and Josh?"

Laurie quirked an eyebrow at her. "Yes. Why are you so surprised?" She shrugged. "They've been dating for months. No big secret. They've been the talk of the station all fire season."

Ashley just sat there with her mouth gaping.

"What's going on?" Laurie took another bite of her sandwich. "You look kind of weird."

"But at your party—" was all Ashley managed to say.

"Oh, yeah. I saw you arrive, and then you were gone. What happened? I tried to wave you down, but maybe you didn't see me." A frown creased her brow. "Were the girls okay? I'm sorry I didn't follow up with a phone call, but I got distracted, and then we were getting ready for our East Coast trip."

Ashley sat back in the booth, lightheaded and shocked. She *knew* what she saw. It had played over and over in her head like a movie reel since that night. Kat cuddled up in Noah's lap. They were smiling and laughing, exchanging desirous glances. Kat with her bright-red lips pouted for a kiss. Her lush figure poured into that gold lamé jumpsuit, red high heels dangling in the air. Noah grinning, fully enjoying holding her in his arms.

Tears flooded her eyes at the memory. A few beads of moisture trickled down her cheeks as she recalled that Noah was always irritated and busy when she called, interrupting something, interrupting *them*. Her stomach turned. Putting down her glass, she held the napkin to her mouth.

"Ashley! What in the world is wrong? You look like you're going to throw up or pass out or both!" Laurie scrutinized her from across the table. "Are you sick? Do you need help?"

Wedging herself out of the booth, Laurie rushed to Ashley's side.

"I'm okay. It's okay." She took a deep breath and sipped her iced tea with trembling hands.

Laurie sat back down in the booth, watching her with a vigilant eye.

Ashley cleared her throat and shared what she witnessed at the party, her voice quivering with emotion. "You should have seen his face, Laurie. He was almost giddy." She pulled a tissue from her purse and wiped her tears. "Now you're telling me Kat and Josh are getting married?" She gave Laurie a dubious stare. "Does Josh realize what's going on with Noah and Kat?"

Laurie's mouth fell open. "*Nothing* is going on with Noah and Kat. You just happened to walk in at the wrong moment and jumped to a conclusion. The wrong conclusion." She scooted over and wrapped her arms around Ashley. "Oh, honey, I wish we had talked sooner. This is all a misunderstanding."

Ashley sniffed. "I *know* what I saw. The picture is engraved in my brain permanently." The vision of Noah and Kat swirled in her head. "Every time I've tried to talk with Noah since the party, he's been distracted and angry, saying he's busy and that I'm bothering him. He moved on and found someone else." Tears dripped down her face.

"Honey, honey, honey," Laurie said in a soothing tone. "Noah is not in love with anyone but *you*. He's been in mourning, miserable, and extremely frustrated."

She turned to look Ashley in the eyes. "What you saw or thought you saw was Kat having one too many drinks without enough food. She tripped in those outrageous high heels and fell into Noah's lap. She spilled her drink all over him. He was trying to help her stand up. Josh was right there, didn't you see him?"

Ashley shook her head, eyes wide in confusion.

"Kat was a drunken mess and even split that ridiculous skin-tight jumpsuit she was wearing. Everyone was laughing to hide their embarrassment, particularly for Josh. He had to quickly cover her with his jacket and take her home." Laurie raised her eyebrows and gave a quick laugh. "I'm sure she had one huge hangover the next day."

Ashley gasped in disbelief. "No way."

Laurie gave her a reassuring smile. "Noah tried to laugh it off, too, but it was obvious he was uncomfortable and had red wine splashed all over him. He left shortly after." Laurie took Ashley's cold hands in hers. "That's what happened, Ashley. That's the truth." She gave her friend an earnest smile. "If I had known what you thought you saw, I would have chased you down the street and all over town, for that matter." She shook her head dramatically. "Kat spilled red wine all over my new white chair and the carpet. It took forever to get the stain out. What a mess."

Ashley laughed. Then snorted. And burst into tears.

Laurie hugged her again and let her cry for a while. "Truthfully, Ashley, Noah loves you, and he wants to make things right. The man is beside himself over your separation, but this crazy fire season hasn't allowed him to process things or given him a chance to make things right."

"I've been so self-centered and self-righteous. I don't know if he'll be able to forgive me." Twisting the tissue nervously, she looked up at Laurie. "Do you think he will?"

"He's out of his mind being away from his family, and now he's dealing with life and death situations." Laurie stared at her with compassion in her eyes. "Give him another chance, my friend. Times have been tough for all of us in emergency services, and our marriages. We all need to lean on each other for support and ask for God's grace during these times."

*****

Ashley chewed on Laurie's words as she drove to the school to pick up Emma and Katie. She was still in disbelief that what she thought she saw wasn't the truth. She had agonized for weeks over the thought of Noah and Kat together, conjuring up all kinds of misconceptions.

It was all a lie…the kind of lie the evil one loved to let fester and destroy relationships, especially a Christian marriage. *God, please protect us. I pray for our marriage to be healed and made even stronger. In Jesus's name. Amen.*

In the pick-up lane, Ashley ran into an old friend from the NICU.

"Hi, Ashley." Jessica waved. "It's been forever. How *are* things?"

Ashley stepped out of the car to chat with her friend. "I'm doing pretty well. How about you?"

"Great! I've been working here as a school nurse for almost four months now. The schedule is wonderful. I love having time off with my family when school's out. We have a boy and a girl now, the same ages as your daughters."

"That's awesome. That schedule sounds *so* nice. I commute an hour each way, but I do love the NICU. How do you like school nursing versus acute care? Do you feel challenged as an RN?"

"I know what you're thinking. Boring, huh? Glorified Band-Aid queen?" Jessica laughed. "That's what I thought, too, but it's a very independent, challenging role. The school nurse is *the* medical professional in an educational setting. If you think about it, an RN's ratio in an acute setting is 1:2 or 1:3. Granted, this isn't acute care, but I'm responsible for monitoring the health of about two thousand students, more and more of them having special health care needs. Some days are quiet with vision and hearing testing and paperwork, but others are crazy with all kinds of accidents, seizures, you name it. A little of everything. Every day is different."

She raised her hands. "The position requires a lot of expertise. I'm getting my master's degree and school nurse credential. It's a requirement for the job, but you have five years to complete it. I go to the college for intensive sessions once a month on the weekends, Friday afternoon through Sunday afternoon. They design the classes for people working full-time in the school setting."

"That's great. Makes it convenient for those who work."

She nodded. "We have a lot of fun too. The group stays at the same hotel, and we go out for dinner and take long walks on the river walkway behind the university on breaks. It's nice being around like-minded people and a good break from the family and kids."

Jessica touched Ashley's shoulder excitedly. "Hey, I just heard of a position opening up that would be perfect for you with your NICU background and leadership skills. A full-time school nurse position working with children with special needs and severe disabilities is opening up in January. They just posted the position. You would be just around the corner from your daughters' school, and on the same schedule."

"Hmm…that would be fantastic!" Ashley's stomach fluttered with excitement.

"The school helps me with tuition. Granted, the pay is less than the hospital, but the hours, benefits, faculty, and students are great. You know the expression, the three best months of teaching are June, July, and August."

She clapped her hands. "I love, love, love having weekends, holidays, and the summer off with my family. Who needs all that stress from the hospital and the administration?"

The final bell rang, and Ashley started to turn toward her car.

"Think about it, Ashley. You would be perfect." Jessica searched her purse and handed her a business card. "Call me if you want to talk more about it. You could probably even shadow the school nurse currently in the position to get more of an idea of the job. Sally is retiring after over twenty-plus years in the position. It's important to her that someone with the right qualifications and heart steps in." She gave Ashley a quick hug. "Wonderful seeing you again."

Jessica wove her way through the flow of students greeting familiar faces. Waiting and watching for the girls, Ashley contemplated the recent events. She had a feeling God was nudging her to seriously consider this potential opportunity. It would certainly make life easier in many ways. She wouldn't miss commuting or the twelve-hour shifts, but would she feel fulfilled?

26

Ashley's mind churned with all the events of the afternoon. *Kat and Josh are getting married this Saturday.* She shook her head to clear her thoughts. Noah still loved her and wasn't having an affair.

She recalled all the weeks of sleepless nights and bad dreams. The anxiety and dark cloud of depression weighing her down, the fear of being abandoned, alone, unwanted and unlovable. *Lies…all lies that I allowed to fester in my heart and soul!*

She spotted Emma and Katie waving at their friends while making their way toward the car. Ashley said a quick prayer of thanksgiving to God for His promises and answers. The words of Jeremiah 29:11 swept through her spirit: *"For I know the plans I have for you, declares the Lord, plans to prosper you and not to harm you, plans to give you hope and a future."*

"Thank you, Lord," Ashley whispered as she turned to greet her precious daughters.

"Hi, girls." She waved as they climbed into the car. "How was your day? I want to hear every little detail."

"I think I aced my English test," Katie beamed.

"We're going to be doing a unit on dance in my gym class," Emma said. "My teacher knows I take dance class and asked if I would be a student co-lead."

Katie hopped up and down on the backseat. "Can Piper spend the night on Friday? Her parents said it was okay."

"Yes, Katie, but next time, please ask me first."

"Okay, sorry."

"Can I have a friend over Friday too?"

"All right, Emma, who do you want to ask?"

"I'm thinking Zoe. We both have jazz and ballet classes on Saturday."

Her heart warmed as she smiled at her girls. "Thoughts on dinner? Something simple like tacos sound good?"

"Yes! And ice cream?"

"Can we rent a movie?"

"Two movies! One for each of us." Emma put her hands in prayer position. "Please?"

Laughing at their earnestness, Ashley relented. "All right, but here's the deal. Tacos and ice cream. Two movies, but I have to approve them, and nothing rated higher than PG. Lights-out and bedtime by 10:00 p.m. Emma, like you mentioned, you have dance classes at 9:00, and Katie, you have a riding lesson at 12:00, and I desperately need some beauty sleep." She held up her hand to high five. "Deal or no deal?"

"Deal!" They both high fived her.

Ashley enjoyed hearing their happy laughter and getting to know their friends. She always wanted to have the cool hangout house where friends and family were welcome.

This is what I want. To be here, fully present, for my girls, for my family. I love the NICU…but this is my life, and my priority. In an instant flash of clarity, Ashley knew what she had to do.

*****

She woke up early the next morning to meditate and pray. *Lord, if this is your purpose and your will that I go into school nursing, I pray YOU would open the doors and show me clearly.*

She wandered downstairs to make a cup of coffee. Then she sat down in front of the computer and applied for the position.

Thy will be done. A sense of peace filled her as she pulled out Jessica's business card, typing out her work e-mail in the recipient line.

In the body of the e-mail, she wrote:

> Jessica, great seeing you yesterday. Been thinking a lot about the special education school

nurse position and just submitted my application. Wondering if you could help me set up that shadow day with the current nurse. Really appreciate the opportunity to see what this job entails in action.

Thanks,
Ashley Smith

The moment, she hit send, Ashley's heart soared with enthusiasm and hope. She hopped on her stationary bike and punched in a thirty-minute country music interval-hills program to start the day.

*****

That evening, Ashley opened a response from Jessica.

Hi Ashley,

I spoke with Sally today and told her all about you and your experience. She was thrilled that you might be interested in the position and would love to meet with you and have you shadow for as long as you would like. Here's her contact information.

Sally

P.S. I ran into the superintendent today and put in a good word for you. If you want the job, I'm pretty sure it's yours. ☺

Ashley sat back in amazement. *God, when you make a move, you don't waste a minute!*

More and more confident and comfortable in her decision, Ashley composed an e-mail to Sally.

Hi Sally,

This is Ashley Smith, Jessica's friend from the NICU. Very interested in arranging a few days to shadow with you. Would next Monday and Tuesday work for you?

I appreciate your time, and thank you in advance.

Ashley

*****

The following Monday, Ashley and Sally spent the day making the rounds of the six classrooms Sally covered. They toured the infant program and observed 1:1 therapy with the teacher, infant, and parent, and attended a group speech therapy session.

In total, Sally was responsible for approximately three hundred students at five different locations. Ashley was amazed at the technology utilized into the classroom setting. All the children in the program, from infant to eighth grade, qualified for the special education program for children with special health care needs.

In one classroom, the children were fully integrated into a regular classroom setting and assisted by an educational aid. Another classroom had children who required skilled nursing care. Their medical needs were met by a licensed vocational nurse or a registered nurse, depending upon severity and what care they needed. There were children with ventilators, feeding tubes, catheters, and all kinds of specialized wheelchairs and equipment.

The school nurse for the special education program for the severely disabled supervised the overall health care needs of the students. Her responsibilities also included oversight of the health care assistants and nursing staff.

Additionally, the school nurse worked in tandem with all the educators and specialists such as speech and language therapists, occupational and physical therapists, and adaptive physical education teachers.

Each student had a small army of specialists working together for their benefit. The special education instructor was the bandleader, making sure the student received all the necessary therapy and accommodations in order to facilitate their learning.

Sally observed Ashley diligently to see how she interacted with the students and how quickly she caught on to the verbiage in the special education setting. She spent time providing Ashley with in-depth explanations of her role. She shared how much she had enjoyed her position for the last twenty-plus years and how her work had positively impacted her life.

On Tuesday, Ashley sat in on an annual IEP meeting for a student with multiple complex health care needs. She was impressed at the amount of detail and knowledge each of the specialized providers offered in their assessment of his progress toward meeting his goals and objectives. The administrator tried to cut back on a few of the services to save money. This was fiercely but gracefully rebuked by the specialists with the parents' approval.

After the IEP meeting, the student's mother came into Sally's office to discuss a new medication her son had been prescribed. *She seems familiar.*

Catching Ashley's gaze, the mom asked, "Do I know you?"

Ashley smiled. "You're familiar to me as well. I've worked in the NICU at Mercy Hospital for quite a few years, probably during the time your son was there. I'm Ashley, by the way."

"Brittney." The mom pointed at herself, a sad cloud crossing her face. "I actually had twins. A boy and a girl…but our daughter didn't live beyond a few hours." Tears sprung to her eyes. She grabbed a tissue from the box on Sally's desk. "It was so hard. My husband and I were in a car accident. He was hospitalized with injuries, and I went into early labor." Her shoulders shook, and her voice cracked.

Ashley had a moment of recognition and was filled with compassion. Recalling the tragic event, she scooted her chair next to Brittney, placing her arm around her shoulder for support. "I'm *so* sorry for your loss. That's heartbreaking."

Brittney tearfully nodded. "I have a question I've always wanted to know the answer to, but I didn't know who to ask." Wiping her eyes again, she looked up expectantly. "Maybe I can ask you?"

Ashley gave her a hug. She felt deeply for everything this poor woman had been through from having premature twins, one not surviving, and the twin who survived needing specialized health care and education for the rest of his life.

Wow, that is really a lot. I never thought beyond saving their lives to what comes afterward.

"Please ask me, and I'll answer if I can."

Brittney's lips tightened, and her voice wavered. "I had an emergency C-section, and there were complications." She twisted the tissue in her hands. "I nearly died of hemorrhaging. My placenta separated from the womb because of the accident."

Ashley nodded her head in understanding.

"Both my husband and I were in surgery when our baby girl passed. Sarah was her name." Tears streamed down her face. "I...I always wondered what happens. Did Sarah die alone on the warming table? Or was someone with her?" Sobs burst out of her chest from a deep, hidden hole in her heart. "Whenever I think of my precious baby girl dying alone—I just can't...stand it. Everything happened so quickly, and none of our family or relatives could get there in time. I just wish with all my heart that I could have been there and tell her how much she was—*is* loved."

Ashley leaned forward, resting both arms lightly on Brittney's shoulders. She knew beyond a doubt that years ago, God had put her in that time and place, and now in this time and place.

She met Brittney's eyes with an honest steadfast look. "I was one of the transport nurses for your babies. I remember them well. A placental abruption isn't common, so it stands out in my mind. All of us in the NICU were so sorry for your heartbreaking loss. I hope your husband is doing all right."

Brittney nodded. "He gimps around a little when the weather is cold, but otherwise, he's fine." Her eyes filled with hope. "You were there?"

"Yes, I had the greatest honor of holding your precious daughter, Sarah, singing lullabies to her and telling her how much she was loved."

Tears streamed down everyone's faces.

"Sarah had the most perfect rosebud mouth and delicate features. A beautiful child. I wrapped her up in warm blankets and held her until she passed and beyond."

Audible sniffling filled the room.

"Several of the nurses helped me make a couple of copies of her hand and footprints and took some photos of her. You got those, didn't you?"

"Yes. They're my greatest treasures. I cherish them." She gave Ashley a watery smile. "Thank you. Without them, it would seem like she never even existed. I look at them all the time and the little hat she wore." Her voice cracked with emotion. "Did she suffer?"

Ashley gave her a gentle hug. "No. Sarah didn't suffer at all. She went right into the arms of God peacefully. I promise you that." She rubbed Brittney's back in slow gentle circles. "I held her and rocked her and sang to her like she was one of my own. She was content and just closed her eyes. I held her for a long time. It was serene and beautiful."

Ashley felt the tension flow out of Brittney's body as if releasing a burden she'd carried for far too long.

"Thank you," she whispered. "I'm so grateful. I've agonized about this in my mind since the twins were born. Now I recognize you from the NICU. You were there during the months my son was hospitalized."

"Yes. I'm a charge nurse in the NICU, so I'm not always at the bedside, but I'm in and out of the unit all day."

Taking Ashley's hands in hers, she shook them gratefully. "Again, thank you. I hope you decide to take this position." She turned to Sally. "She would be the perfect fit."

Sally nodded. "Agreed."

Brittney and Sally finished their discussion about the boy's medication. Then she turned and smiled. Her eyes were reddened with emotion, but there was also an aura of peacefulness.

"Thank you." She walked out of the school nurse office with a lightness in her step.

"Wow," Sally said, "that was truly a God thing."

Ashley nodded. She knew how thoughts and untruths could fester until they seemed to be reality. She sent a prayer of thanksgiving to God for freeing her from the bondage of untruths and for putting her in a position to comfort Brittney.

At the end of the school day, she thanked Sally for her time and for sharing her expertise.

"Great. Let me know if any questions come up." She gave Ashley a quick hug. "I think you would be perfect and wish you the best."

Walking to the parking lot, Ashley smiled at the children lined up for their bus ride home. Her heart warmed. They weren't just children with disabilities but fighters and survivors.

As she drove to the girls' school to pick them up, her heart quickened at the thought of talking to Noah, sharing this new possibility with him, and most importantly, asking him to move back home and work on their marriage.

27

Noah was bone tired. This was his fourteenth day in a row as the operations chief working in the Incident Command Post. It was non-stop pressure. Hard, fast, and important decisions had to be made. The tactical radios chattered and squawked in the background, alerting the ICP to new flare-ups as fatality numbers and property destruction counts continued to mount. The phones rang nonstop, the tension tangible. Fingers were pointing blame as the firefighters valiantly tried to control the wind-driven blazes. It was an unprecedented and seemingly impossible battle.

He pulled his headphones off and motioned to his coworkers that he was taking a break. Stepping outside, he rolled his neck in an effort to release tension. Sleep had been fitful, broken up by frequent alerts. He couldn't recall ever feeling so frazzled and fatigued. It was getting harder and harder to focus. Their only saving grace was the prediction of a pineapple express storm from the Gulf of Mexico expected to hit tomorrow. Hopefully, the storm would bring enough moisture to make a significant impact on the fires burning statewide. The concern was that these storms were often preceded by strong wind shears, making fire activity squirrely and unpredictable.

He pulled out his phone and scrolled through his messages. He noticed a few missed calls from Ashley and a voice mail. The first part of her message talked about quitting her job and accepting a position as a school nurse. His brow knitted, and he shook his head. *What? She loves her job.*

Her message continued: "Noah, I'm so sorry for the way I've acted. I've been selfish and self-serving, and I apologize. I'm hoping and praying we can work through this. If you're available, the girls and I would like you to come over for dinner on Christmas Eve. I'll make a special dinner, and we can exchange gifts, like before. I do love you. Sorry if I made you doubt that. Please be safe and call when you can. Bye."

Puzzled, Noah ended the voice mail. He had been badly hurt and was afraid to trust her again. He didn't think his heart could take more pain. Plus, he was just too dog-tired to go on an emotional roller coaster. He pocketed his phone and headed back inside. He needed time to sort this out before calling her back.

*****

As predicted, the storm blew in with a vengeance. High winds swirled up the warlike scenes of harried evacuations through raining veils of flame. Many died while fleeing in their cars. The firestorm overran them. The body count continued to rise. There weren't enough resources, and the firefight got away from those who were trying to fight it. Several more firefighters lost their lives, trapped on the ridges with walls of flame bearing down.

Radios crackled.

"This is Hotshot Crew Four. We're trapped on the west facing ridge. Please send assistance. There are twenty-three of us."

Noah closed his eyes, rubbing his face in torment. The agonizing pleas for help continued to come across the radios. Except there was no help. The pleas turned into panicked cries…then silence.

Pacing the room, Noah ground his teeth in frustration.

Please, Lord, let the rains begin. There was no other hope. The situation was now beyond human intervention. They needed a miracle.

And then the miracle came. The pineapple express, true to its name. Torrents of rain followed the initial wind shears, dousing hillsides one range at a time. However, the answered prayer was also a curse. Torrential rains brought in new concerns of mudslides and flooding. The hillsides had been stripped of the natural vegetation to hold back the dirt. And the storm sat, saturating the barren ridge tops the fire had recently ravaged. The fire crews now fought a new battle against the destructive force of water.

*****

Ashley anxiously waited for Noah's call. None came. She called again twice and left messages, each more concerned for his safety and well-being. "Noah, please call or text me back, even if it's just to let me know you're okay. I know you're busy, but I'm concerned about you."

Putting her phone on vibrate, she hurried into her supervisor's office for their meeting. "Hi, Michelle. Thanks for meeting with me."

"Of course. Anytime." Michelle motioned for Ashley to sit and gestured toward the electric kettle and basket of assorted teas. "Would you like some tea?"

"Oh, that sounds great." Ashley pulled a decaf Earl Grey from the selection.

Michelle handed her a steaming mug of water and Ashley plunked her tea bag into it, nervously tugging the tea bag string up and down. She wanted this conversation to end on a good note and not burn any bridges.

"You wanted to discuss something?" Michelle began.

Ashley took a sip of tea, then began to explain the events preceding their meeting. The chance encounter with Jessica, the available school nurse position, her experience shadowing, and her desire to make changes based on their family needs and fire season.

"So I think I have to tender my resignation. I appreciate the opportunity and the experience I've gained over the past decade. Seriously, you've been wonderful. Thank you for everything. Right now, I just need to do the best thing for my family and our situation."

Michelle leaned forward, an earnest expression on her face. "You've been such an important member of our team, Ashley. You will be greatly missed. But I totally understand the pressure you're under. I just want what's best for you and your family."

Ashley let out a pent-up sigh of relief. "Thank you. I'll miss you and this place so much."

"What's your time frame for leaving? You'll be hard to replace."

"I appreciate that. I just found out they offered me the position, so we have some time. The current school nurse is retiring at the end of the school year, and they would like me to start March first, so she can train and transition me into the position."

"Let's see, it's almost Christmas, so about eight weeks." Michelle clapped her hands. "Perfect. Thank you for the notice. That helps."

Ashley reached into her briefcase and pulled out her typed letter of resignation. "Now it's official. Whew! I was sweating that."

She finished her last swallow of tea and shook Michelle's hand, sincerely looking into her supervisor's eyes. "Thank you. God bless you and everyone in the NICU. I'll miss it terribly."

"You will be missed as well. Please say hi to Jessica from me. I'm glad to hear she is doing well and enjoying her job. Just tell her not to steal anymore of my staff." With a wink, she continued, "Just kidding. I'm happy for both of you."

Tears misted in Ashley's eyes as she turned to leave. Glancing at the clock, she saw it was already 5:00. Emma and Katie were spending the night at their friends, Emma at Zoe's, and Katie at Piper's. It was Friday night.

It'll be nice to have some time to myself. Maybe I'll stop and pick up something for dinner, then a good book and a bubble bath. Relieved the meeting with Michelle had gone so smoothly, she felt herself starting to relax. She pulled her coat tighter around her body and stepped out into the chilling winter fog.

Just outside the hospital entrance, she almost tripped over a pair of legs. She looked down to see a body lying face down, seemingly lifeless, in a pool of blood. She screamed. "Rodney!"

28

Ashley dropped to her knees to feel for Rodney's vitals. He barely had a pulse and was breathing shallowly. Rolling him over, she tilted his head to open his airway. Red blotches stained the front of his uniform. There were multiple stab wounds on his chest and stomach.

"Rodney! Can you hear me?"

His eyes fluttered.

She placed her hand in his palm. "Squeeze my hand if you can hear me."

His fingers curled weakly around her hand. Breathing a sigh of relief, she whipped off her coat to cover him from the cold. She stuffed her purse under his legs to elevate them as she hastily formulated a plan. *It would be quicker to run back inside and get help than to call 911.*

"Rodney, I'm going to get help. Squeeze again if you hear me and understand." He squeezed weakly. "I'll be right back with help. Okay?" She felt another slight pressure on her hand.

He struggled to open his eyes. And when he did, they got more wide-eyed. Strong arms grabbed her from behind and yanked her to her feet. A hand slapped over her mouth. Gagging on the filthy odor, Ashley was dragged to the staff entrance, kicking and fighting as hard as she could. The man strong-armed her and zip tied her arms behind her. He ripped her ID from her uniform, swiped it, and pushed her through the door, a knife to her throat.

"You're going to get me drugs!" he snarled as he fisted the front of her scrubs and pulled her through the door. It shut and locked automatically behind her.

Ashley stared at her attacker, an obviously strung-out man in his early twenties. A baseball cap and hoodie covered his head and hung on his wiry frame. There was a feral look in his eyes.

"Where are the drugs, lady? I'm going to cut you if you don't get me drugs!" He pressed the knife more firmly to her throat.

A trickle of warm blood ran down her neck.

Ashley prayed. She had to get help for Rodney! *Stay calm. Be smart about this. You're only going to get one chance.*

"Okay, I'll get you drugs." She tried to keep her quavering voice steady.

The zip ties bit into her flesh. He pushed her down the hallway, the steely point now pressed into her back. The rattle of a housekeeping cart echoed ahead. He shoved her to an empty linen room. She stumbled, almost falling. He pulled her up straight by her arms. The cart rattled by without stopping.

"What kind of drugs do you want?" she needed to keep him talking.

He jerked her around to face him and put the blade to her throat again.

"You know what I'm looking for…you're a nurse. Morphine, fentanyl, oxycontin. Where's the pharmacy?" he growled.

"It's just down that hallway." She motioned with a jerk of her head.

"Don't play games with me, lady. I'll do to you what I did to that guard outside."

Her mind raced, hastily putting together a plan. "I'm not playing games. I'm getting you drugs."

He dragged her to the door of the room and scanned the corridor. Yanking her out into the hallway, knife again at her back, he swore, "Quit messing around and show me now, last chance before I kill you."

This was her only chance. She stepped into an empty patient room and hit the light switch.

He followed, knife at the small of her back.

"The public doesn't know this, but in every patient room, we have a locked supply of pain medications. It's hidden next to the linen supplies."

"Show me. You'd better not be lying." He pushed her ahead of him, the knife tip piercing the back of her uniform.

She winced as the blade broke her skin.

Her fear gave way to mounting anger. She was not going to allow this thug to ruin her life or Rodney's. She was ready to fight for them both. Thoughts of her daughters and Noah whirled.

Not on my watch! God is with me and for me. My strength comes from the Lord. God, please send your mighty angels to fight this battle. Give me strength and courage!

The man got more wild-eyed, his movements jerky and unpredictable. "Show me the cabinet. Now!" He pressed harder with the knife. The pain was becoming excruciating. Blood soaked through her scrubs.

"I have to have my hands free to open it."

"Why?" He gave her a menacing scowl.

"Because each medication lock opens with our index fingerprints for security. Not everyone has access to narcotics...but I do."

He jerked her neck and pushed his knee hard into her back. "Be straight with me," he hissed, his breath fetid and hot.

"I am." Her heart raced with anticipation. Nausea twisted her gut.

With a swipe of the knife, he cut the zip ties, nicking her wrists in the process. Ashley rubbed her sore and bleeding wrists while slowly walking to the supposed hidden cabinet. Suddenly, she turned, grabbed the bedside table, and ran forward, ramming it as hard as she could into the man, sending him sprawling on the ground. The knife shot across the room, spinning wildly. She ran behind the bed to the wall panel and hit the Code Blue button. Before the man could get up, she kicked the knife out into the hallway.

The loudspeaker suddenly announced.

"Code Blue, Room 342. Code Blue, Room 342. Code Blue, Room 342."

Within seconds, the room would be swarmed with Code Blue Team members.

The man lunged at her. "You lied!" He shouted profanity and tried to grab her throat.

She kicked out, hitting him in the groin. He dropped to the floor again, screaming.

Members of the Code Blue Team arrived on the scene.

Ashley quickly explained the scenario. "Rodney is by the staff entrance door! He has multiple stab wounds and is bleeding out. Hurry!"

Several of the team members held the man down until security arrived.

Laurie flew into the room, throwing her arms around Ashley. "Are you okay? I was on shift and heard what happened." Seeing the wounds on her neck, wrists, and blood-soaked back, she hugged her tighter. "You are one brave woman, sister. Let's get you cleaned up and bandaged."

God, thank you for sending your angels and giving me strength and courage. She had no doubt God had answered her prayers.

*****

Many hours later, after filing a police report, having her wounds treated and bandaged, receiving a dose of IV antibiotics, showering and changing into clean scrubs, she went to visit Rodney. Emergency surgery had successfully stopped his internal bleeding. He had just gotten out of the recovery room and was settled in his ICU bed. Blood transfusions were infusing into both arms. His wife and grandson were at his side.

"Ashley," Rodney whispered, his voice weak. "How can I thank you for saving my life? I'm the one who's supposed to be protecting yours."

She leaned down and kissed his cheek. "Thank the Lord. That's who saved us both."

She wrapped his wife, Ruth, in a hug and admired their sleeping grandson. After a short visit with promises to stop by again tomorrow, Ashley yawned and headed for home. A security guard escorted her to her car. The area around the staff entrance was now buzzing with police and security team members. She thanked her escort and immediately locked her door before starting up the car.

*****

Noah stood and stretched his aching back and neck. After three and a half weeks of nonstop grind, he was finally being released from the incident. *What a mess. First the fire and then the flooding.* He'd never experienced anything like this, which was saying a lot. Noah had been doing some heavy thinking during the wee hours of the morning when, despite how exhausted he was, sleep evaded him. He thought of his work, Ashley, Katie, Emma, and how time was marching along with or without him. He missed his family dreadfully, the individuals as well as everything family and home stood for—love, laughter, companionship, a future.

Driving the long route home from the fire, Noah visualized various scenarios and how best to approach them. He called Ashley to let her know he was heading back. She told him about her experience at the hospital.

"Wow! I'm so thankful you're okay...and Rodney. You were so brave. I'm proud of you. But I'm not surprised either, you're one tough woman. You have to be to be married to a firefighter."

"Thanks, but it's the Lord who deserves the credit. He wants us to be a whole family again."

Emotion rasped his voice. "I want that too. I can't wait until you're in my arms again."

"Me, too, Noah...me too. Come home to us."

"I'll be there as soon as I can. Just have to fill out some forms and documents from the fire first. Then I'll be done and off for a few days. I love you all. See you tomorrow."

He pulled into the command center, so tired he could barely formulate words, and rapped on his supervisor's door.

"Enter!" a rough voice responded.

He stepped inside the office and closed the door behind him. "Chief Hickam? Do you have a few minutes?"

His crotchety old supervisor motioned toward the chair in front of his desk. "Sit."

Settling down in the office chair, Noah cleared his dry throat, not eager to aggravate his boss but steadfast in his mission. "I wanted to tell you that I'd like to officially withdraw from my command team duties. With climate change and fire season now year-round and nonstop, it's too much time away from my family. My marriage and relationship with my girls are suffering because of it. I sincerely appreciate the opportunity, and I'm willing to stay on the teams until I'm replaced. However, I respectfully wish to be released from both teams to focus on my Air Attack responsibilities."

Noah sat back, his body tense as he waited for his boss's response. Chief Hickam was difficult and known to ruin subordinates' careers.

His supervisor gave him an appraising look. He rubbed the bridge of his nose with a gnarled finger, his voice lowering to a rough growl. "As your boss, I should say no. Don't do it. It's a bad decision for your career and future." Pausing, he gave Noah a steely gaze. Abruptly, an unexpected tender look crossed his weathered face. "Son, I wish I'd had the courage to do what you're doing many years ago. If I had, I would probably still be happily married instead of a lonely old fireman."

Noah stared at the chief in surprise. This was a soft side of him no one had seen before.

"But as someone who knows what happens when you put career before family, I think you're making the right decision." He patted his hand over his heart and gave Noah a wink. "Put your heart and your family first. Nobody ever stands at the pearly gates and says, 'I really wish I'd worked harder.'"

Noah stood up and shook his hand. "Thank you, sir. Well-spoken advice."

Chief Hickam wrinkled his sharp blue eyes in amusement. "Give your wife an extra hug and kiss from me. You can e-mail me your resignation from the command teams."

Noah smiled back in relief. "Yes, sir. Thank you, sir."

As he walked out of the office, the tension melted from his shoulders. For the first time in a very long time, he felt a sense of peace.

Tomorrow was Christmas Eve. He couldn't wait to see his family, enjoy a home-cooked meal, and celebrate the holiday together. For now, he looked forward to a long hot shower and a full night's sleep. Whistling a tune, he started his work vehicle and headed to his apartment.

29

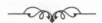

Ashley bustled around the kitchen, Christmas music played in the background. The house was filled with the holiday spirit with the sharp bite of fresh cut pine from their tree in the living room, colorful wrapped presents piled high under its decorated branches. The sweet smell of apple cider and cinnamon sticks wafted. A red velvet cake with cream cheese frosting sat in a glass covered cake dish on the counter.

Katie and Emma were beside themselves to see their dad, running in and out of the kitchen to lick the frosting off the beaters and snatching tastes of grated cheese and other tidbits. Sensing the excitement, Callie, Nikki, and Trina circled the kitchen and living room.

"How much longer till Dad's here?" Katie asked for the fourth time.

Ashley glanced at the clock. "About thirty minutes. Enough time for you and Emma to finish all your chores and set the table."

Katie gave her an exaggerated courtesy. "At your service, Madam."

Ashley slid the ham into the oven to warm.

The Casting Crowns song, "Broken Together," played on the radio. The words tugged at her heart, and she paused to listen carefully. She was moved by the Holy Spirit speaking to her through the song.

Tears welled as memories of the abandonment and anger she felt with every missed birthday, anniversary, and other important events flashed though her mind.

She wiped her tears on the hand towel. *Only you can heal this marriage, Lord. Please help us to seek you first in all of our decisions, thoughts, and actions.*

Broken together. That's how we heal this marriage with broken humility with who we are now...with all our imperfections and blisters. Help me to lay down fairy tales and fantasies of what a marriage should be and focus on the perfect mate you've chosen for me. Help me to be the wife Noah needs, for us to love who we are and what each of us bring to this marriage and family. Thank you, Lord.

She rinsed the sink and went to freshen up before Noah arrived. The girls were finishing their chores and setting the table. A sense of peace engulfed her with her decision to leave the NICU for the school nurse position. God, family, and then career.

Confident Noah would agree with her decision, she brushed her teeth, dabbed on a bit of the J'adore perfume he had given her for her birthday, and freshened her lip-gloss. The doorbell rang, and her heart raced.

His arrival was met with a flurry of activity. Emma and Katie threw their arms around his waist as the dogs barked, thumping their tails on the entry floor. Trina meowed, jumping up to the top of her cat tree to gain a better view.

"Wow! That's the homecoming I've been waiting for." He turned to Ashley with a nervous smile. "Hi," he whispered.

She opened her arms wide. "Welcome home."

*****

Noah stepped into Ashley's arms, and his world felt complete. Lifting her off her feet, he twirled, drawing her close. The girls laughed and cheered.

Ashley tightened her arms around him and kissed him firmly on the lips. He kissed her back, the angst of the past few months melting away, replaced with love and contentment. The dogs barked, leaping up around them. Trina waved her paws in the air, seeking attention.

He set Ashley down and gazed around the room, reaching out to pet Trina. "Wow! It's so awesome to be home."

"It's amazing to have you home. We've missed you so much. Thank God you are here safe and sound."

Noah smiled at her tenderly. "Dinner smells delicious. I've been dreaming about your home-cooked meals after eating fire camp food and MREs for weeks."

Ashley stepped in for one longer hug. "Dinner will be ready in about ten minutes. I made all your favorites as promised."

He rubbed his stomach in anticipation. "Hey, girls, give me a hand with the Christmas gifts in my car."

The girls rushed out to help bring in the presents. Noah had been busy all day buying and wrapping gifts. He vowed to make more of an effort to celebrate and participate in these family times. Later, he and Ashley could hash out some finer details, and he could tell her about his decision to resign from the command teams. He wanted to hear more about her decision to leave the hospital. *Lots of changes…but for the best and for their family.*

The girls' laughter bounced off the walls as they stomped the snow off their boots and settled the gifts under the tree. His heart warmed with the sound of their cheerful banter. *Our family together and a white Christmas. God is good…always.*

They gathered around the table, holding hands and bowing their heads.

Noah prayed. "Thank you, Lord, for all of your blessings, for safety, for our marriage and family, for forgiveness and hope for the future, for the birth of your son, Jesus, whom we celebrate tonight, and for your gift of salvation. Amen."

He gave Ashley's hand an extra squeeze. "I missed all of you so much."

Ashley gazed into Noah's eyes with a watery smile. "It's where you belong. Where we all belong together as a family."

Hours later, after dinner, dessert, and unwrapping of gifts, the girls played contently with their new toys. The dogs and Trina were curled up snoozing by the fireplace. Ashley and Noah sat on the couch holding hands. Leaning down for kiss, Noah looked longingly into her eyes. "I'd like to stay here. Is that okay?"

She wrapped her arms around his neck and kissed him back. "This is your home and where you should be. I want you to stay."

"I want to wake up with you in my arms. Let's not get into a big discussion about the future. It can wait until tomorrow or later. Let's just enjoy now."

"Agreed. I'm going to take these dessert plates into the kitchen to soak." Standing, she turned and smiled lovingly at her husband. "Be right back."

Noah grabbed some dishes and followed her into the kitchen. Setting them in the sink, he looked up at the clock. "I think I'll run over to the apartment and pick up some clothes and toiletries. I'll be back in a flash. Okay? We can enjoy Christmas morning together."

"Okay. Hurry back!" Glancing out the window she frowned. "It's getting pretty foggy out there. Be careful."

Kissing her soundly, he grabbed his keys and strode into the night. "Always, babe. Love you."

*****

Noah pulled into his apartment parking spot and sprung out of the car. With powerful strides, he leapt up the steps to the second story. Stuffing a few items into a bag, he switched off the lights and locked the door. *After the holiday, I'll give notice. But I'm not sleeping one more night in this place.* In a hurry to get back home to his family, he skipped down the stairs and threw his bag in the truck.

On alert, he turned on his fog lights and entered the freeway well below the speed limit. Still, he could only see about twenty feet in front. Two miles from home, he saw a car on the side of the road with flashing hazard lights on. Slowing, he determined that it was an elderly gentleman with a flat tire. He pulled over and approached the vehicle.

The man rolled down his window.

"Merry Christmas," Noah said. "I'm an off-duty firefighter. Need help?"

"Bless you, son. I'm getting too old to handle changing a tire. I called for a tow truck, but they said it would be several hours. Being a holiday and all, they're shorthanded."

"No worries. I'm going to set out safety cones and flares to alert upcoming traffic." The man reached for the car handle. Noah thrust out a hand to stop him. "Please, sir, allow me. It's best if you wait in your car and stay warm. I'll get this done and have you back on the road in no time."

"Thank you," he replied as he rubbed his bony hands together and blew on them.

"Keep your headlights and hazard lights on, okay?"

The man nodded and rolled up his window.

As a firefighter, Noah was always prepared and made sure Ashley had emergency equipment as well. She often joked that she had so much emergency gear—a go bag, fire extinguisher, first aid kit, jumper cables, and so forth—that she had hardly room in the trunk for groceries.

Noah opened his trunk and set out the orange luminescent safety cones, then expertly lit several flares, and set them in front of and behind their cars. He placed the jack under the car and wrestled off the lug nuts. After lifting off the flat tire, he replaced it with the spare. Satisfied everything was secure, he grasped the jack and lug wrench, stood, and turned to put them back in the trunk.

All of a sudden, bright headlights shone and kept coming. At the moment of impact, his world went dark.

30

The doorbell rang. Ashley flung open the front door eager to have Noah home. "Welcome home, Noah."

Her face fell when she instead found her best friend Laurie and her husband, David, fully dressed in his firefighter turnout gear, standing in the doorway.

"What's going on?"

Laurie's face was streaked with tears. David had a stoic stern expression, his turnouts splashed with blood.

Her heart filled with terror. "Noah?" Seeing Laurie's quavering chin and grief-stricken eyes, Ashley covered her face with her hands. "*No! No!*"

The girls came running to the door. Their golden retrievers, Nikki and Calli, frantically barked and ran around the room. Their cat, Trina, swished her tail as her nose twitched, sensing the room.

Emma gripped her mom's arm. "What's going on? Where's Dad?"

Laurie and David stepped into the living room and closed the front door. The girls turned toward them.

Katie's eyes grew wide. "Laurie, why are you crying?"

"Is that blood?" Emma's voice grew increasingly loud and shrill.

Laurie gathered both girls in her arms. "I am so sorry."

Emma shook her head. "Why? Tell us!"

Ashley sobbed in anguish. "This can't be happening!"

Tears streamed down both girls' faces as the reality hit that something bad had happened.

David took command of the situation. "Let's all go into the living room and sit down. Ashley, girls, please come." He waved them into the next room.

Ashley stumbled toward the living room, shock taking hold. Laurie grabbed her hand to steady her and steered her to the couch.

Sitting down, Ashley stared at David through tear-filled eyes. "Is he dead?"

Emma and Katie gasped, holding each other tightly.

"He's not dead, but it's touch and go. I was on battalion coverage tonight when the call came. It appeared as if Noah was headed over here?"

Ashley nodded, her face drawn and anxious. "I've been expecting him for some time now. He just ran over to his apartment to grab a few things. He's moving back home." She let out a moan. "What happened?"

"The accident happened just a few miles away on the freeway. Noah had stopped to help an elderly gentleman change a flat tire." David swallowed roughly.

Ashley rubbed her hands over her face. *That sounds like something he would do.*

"He was just finishing when a passing car hit him. It's really foggy out there, but Noah had set out flares and reflection cones. The disabled car's headlights and hazards were on. He did everything right." He took a deep inhalation. "Ashley, it was a hit and run." Anguish creased his face. "I...I was the first on scene."

Ashley's world crumpled as she closed her eyes, imagining the worst. Her voice shook. "How bad is it?"

"I'm not gonna sugarcoat it. Both femurs are fractured, and he has a severe head injury. He's currently being life-flighted to West General Hospital. The flight nurses suspect that he may have a spinal cord injury, but we don't know for sure." David drew an unsteady breath as Laurie put her arm around his shoulders. "I did everything I could, Ashley, all the responders did. It's in God's hands now."

Ashley fell to her knees in front of David, tears streaming down both of their faces. She clasped his trembling hands and looked straight into his tortured eyes. "Thank you, David. I know you did.

God put you there in that exact spot and time to be there for Noah." Her chin quivered.

She stood, went over to the girls, and wrapped her arms around them. They held on tight, shoulders shaking with their sobs. Ashley looked upward. "We need to pray."

Everyone nodded solemnly, closing their eyes with bowed heads.

She prayed, "Lord Jesus, please help us in our time of need. Give the doctors, nurses, and medical personnel wisdom, discernment, and strength. Help us, Father, to be strong, clear-minded, and steadfast. Thank you for David and Laurie, for their friendship, and David's bravery. I pray we would all lean on your goodness, love, and mercy. In the precious and powerful name of Jesus. Amen."

Ashley paced around the living room. Suddenly, she felt a strong sense of urgency. She turned to her friends. "I have to go to him now! Laurie, could you possibly stay with the girls or take them to your house?"

Laurie walked over to Ashley and pulled her in for a hug. "Go. I'll stay here and take care of the girls and the animals. The boys are at my parents' house. Be with your husband. He needs you."

"Thank you," she whispered softly, hugging her back.

"We want to go see Dad too. Please, Mom." Tears slipped down Emma's cheeks.

"Yeah, we want to go too," Katie pleaded.

Ashley sank to her knees, putting her hands on their shoulders. "I love you both so much, and I know how hard this is on all of us. But right now, I need to go by myself."

As their voices raised in protest, she held up a hand for silence. "I promise you I will call and give you updates. The best thing you can do right now is stay here with Laurie and pray for Dad."

"Okay. We'll stay," Katie said. Emma agreed and slipped her arm around Katie's waist.

"Thank you. I love you, and so does Dad." She turned to Laurie. "I'm going to pack an overnight bag."

In the bedroom, Ashley shoved clothing and toiletry items into her overnight bag and rushed back into the kitchen. "David, I'm ready."

"Why don't you follow me in my fire vehicle? I'd like to swing by the hospital, too, and check on him."

Laurie interjected, "David, she's in no condition to be driving, especially in the fog."

He raised his hands, powerless. "But I'm on call until tomorrow morning. I have to respond if I get dispatched. We'll have to take separate cars or…is there someone you could call to drive you?"

"There's no time for that. I'll be fine," Ashley said. "We need to leave now!"

David gave Laurie a quick nod. "Okay, let's go. Turn on your fog lights and stay close."

"I will." She bent to hug both girls. "I'll call you, okay?"

Somber, they nodded.

She grabbed her keys from the key rack. David's cell phone rang.

"Just a sec, it's the hospital." He answered. "This is Chief Jones speaking." Listening intent for a moment, he turned to Ashley. "His condition has taken a downward turn."

Ashley covered her mouth with her hand, drawing in a breath. "What happened?"

"I don't know the details, but it doesn't sound good. Let's go."

They hustled out the door into the cold foggy Christmas Eve night.

31

Ashley peered through the thick fog as she followed David's fire vehicle. It was claustrophobic, a gray veil engulfing and dampening everything, the normally short ride to the local hospital endless. Her hands dampened as she white-knuckled the wheel.

She rolled down the window and tilted her head, listening for any sound to indicate her pathway. Feeling like she was in an ethereal dream, more like a nightmare, her mind swirled with thoughts of their planned family reunion, renewing their vows, and the devastating news of Noah's accident. Her heart pounded as she visualized him in the ICU on life support. His injuries were life-threatening and his condition deteriorating. Panic seized her as the fog thickened around her.

"I can't see!" Squinting, she could barely make out the soft red glow of David's taillights. She took a steadying breath. "Please, God, let Noah make it. Surround him with your angels and protection. Strengthen him to fight the battle. In Jesus's name, amen." The dash lit up with a phone call flashing. "Incoming call, David Jones."

She hit the answer button. "What's up?"

"Ashley, I got an alert from the other covering battalion chief that there's an accident ahead. He was first on scene and is handling the incident. Sounds like several injuries, possible fatalities. Road's blocked. I notified the highway patrol of our situation, and they'll let us through the accident scene. I'm turning on my Code Three lights…follow me closely. Just so you know, I'm up for the next dispatch call."

"Okay, got it."

Ahead the fog was extenuated by flashing blue and red emergency lights. An officer flagged them by, directing his flashlight around the tangle of piled cars. She followed David through the ghastly sight, weaving around pieces of twisted steel and broken glass. Tendrils of fog hovered over the scene, casting an eerie ghost-like glow. They passed by bloodied bodies and body parts strewn on the pavement. Ashley gasped in horror, her stomach lurching.

The sound of cutting steel and grating of the jaws of life thundered as fire personnel struggled to free those still trapped. She could hear screams and the faint crying of a baby, saw a woman holding a sobbing toddler sat on the ground, looking dazed, smelled the stench of a pungent blood and gasoline mixture seeped into the car and stung her nostrils. Being a nurse, she felt a tugging to stop and render aid, but the thought of Noah barely clinging to life strengthened her resolve to press on toward the hospital.

The flashing lights in her rearview mirror faded as David shut off his emergency lights. They sped down the freeway as fast as they safely could in the blinding fog. Ashley tried not to imagine the horrific scene of Noah being struck. A sob rose in her throat. *Please, God, please.* Finally, the bright lights of the hospital came into view. She swung into a parking space in the visitor's parking lot.

Ashley pulled her overnight bag over her right shoulder and slung her purse across her other shoulder. David took her arm and led her toward the main entrance. A decorated Christmas tree greeted them. Cheerful carols played softly in the background.

"Merry Christmas!" A kind-appearing woman with a hospital nametag that read "Terry" smiled at them from the visitor's desk.

"Merry Christmas," Ashley replied quietly.

Ashley saw the woman's gaze traveling from her tear-streaked face to David's bloodied uniform. Terry's smile faded. Her voice filled with sympathy. "How can I help you, dear?"

Ashley's composure crumpled. She snatched a tissue from the box on the counter and dabbed her eyes. "My husband, Noah Smith, was in a horrible accident tonight. He's in the ICU."

"Oh my. I'm so sorry." A frown shadowed her face. She tapped the computer keys and studied the screen. "Yes, he's in bed seven, fourth floor ICU."

She handed them each visitor tags and gestured toward the elevator. "Take that elevator to the fourth floor and turn right. Ring the buzzer and tell them who you are. They'll allow you access."

As they walked to the elevator, Terry called after them., "I'm notifying the ICU to give them a heads-up you're on your way. I'm praying for you and your family."

"Thanks." Ashley waved as they entered the elevator. She closed her eyes and let her head fall back against the wall, mentally preparing to see her injured husband. "Please, God, help me be strong."

David placed a hand on her back as they arrived at the fourth floor, and the elevator opened with a ding.

"You're tough," David said reassuringly. "Next to Laurie, you're the toughest woman I know."

She gave him a watery smile and punched the intercom ICU button.

"ICU. How can I help you?"

Clearing her throat, she rasped back, "This is Ashley Smith. My husband, Noah, is in bed seven."

"We've been expecting you. Please enter."

A buzzer sounded, and the double doors slowly swung open. They entered and approached the nurse's station. The brightly illuminated ICU was a beehive of activity. Ashley was used to the intensive care setting, but this was so *different*…being the family to a loved one instead of the care provider. She wiped her perspiring palms on her pant leg and brushed a lock of hair away from her face.

A serious-looking man in blue scrubs with a stethoscope around his neck and various bandage scissors, clamps, and rolls of clear tape attached to his hip pouch approached them. He shook both their hands firmly. "I'm Matt, the lead RN taking care of your husband since his arrival."

Ashley wrapped her arms around herself to steady her shaking limbs.

He motioned to a couple of chairs in an alcove. "Please have a seat. Let's talk for a few minutes."

Ashley sank into the chair, her knees bouncing impatiently. "Let's make this quick. I *have* to see him. By the way, I'm an RN, and this is our close friend, David." She touched David's shoulder. "He's a battalion chief and paramedic and was the first to arrive at the scene."

Matt sat down across from them. "Okay, got it. Just let me give you a quick rundown of your husband's status." A deep furrow appeared on his forehead. "He's in very critical condition. Both of his femurs have open fractures, and he has a closed head injury. He's lost a lot of blood, and his blood pressure keeps dropping. We're transfusing as quickly as we can and have him on vasopressors. He's intubated on 100 percent oxygen, and the critical care intensivist, Dr. Fisher, ordered for him to be put in a medically induced coma. We're awaiting the results of the CT scan, but preliminary results indicate severe brain swelling. Good news is that spinal injury has been ruled out. Dr. Fisher will be talking with you as soon as we get more information." Matt paused and looked at Ashley and David. "It's *very* touch and go. Whoever hit him was going fast."

Ashley covered her face with her hands, her back heaving. "How could someone do this…and just leave?"

David gently patted her back. "People who are scared *or* have something to hide run."

She pinched the bridge of her nose between her forefingers. Then she stood resolutely. "Thanks, Matt. I appreciate the info and all of your care, but now I *absolutely have* to see him!"

Matt nodded and motioned for them to follow him down the brightly lit hallway. Passing the bustling nursing station, they turned left to enter room seven.

There was Noah, motionless, except for the rhythmic rise and fall of his chest.

Ashley stood at the doorway. It took her several moments to take it all in. The room was packed with life-support equipment. The ventilator whooshed. Beeping monitors and expansion and release of the air mattress filled the room with mechanical sounds. A row of IV pumps and tubing lined the side of his bed. Blood transfusions infused into IV sites on both arms. Various medications and IV fluids pumped into other sites. Both of Noah's legs were wrapped in bandages and in traction. An intubation tube attached to the ventilator was taped to his mouth, face bruised and swollen beyond recognition. Two bolts bored into his temples were connected to lines measuring the pressure inside his skull.

Ashley rushed to his side, gently placing one of his hands in hers. Matt pulled up chairs for her and David to sit bedside.

"I'll be back in a few. Hit the call button if you need anything." Matt scanned all the monitors before exiting the room.

Leaning forward, she tenderly kissed Noah's hand. "I'm here, Noah. It's Ashley." She squeezed his fingers. "I love you."

He lay unresponsive as the ventilator pumped oxygen into his lungs.

"I'm here too, buddy." David gently patted his arm. "God's got this. You're going to be all right. I know you, man. You're a fighter, and you have a lot to live for." Tears welled and splashed down his cheeks. "Everyone is praying for you. Lots of prayer warriors, all night and all day. Dig deep, dude…fight!" Wiping his tears with open palms, he turned to Ashley, his chin quivering with emotion. "The captain at the fire station is already organizing a blood drive in Noah's name. He put out an e-mail to firefighters from all over the state."

"Thank you." She absently rubbed a spot on Noah's arm where there wasn't an IV line. "Lots of tragedy out there tonight and on Christmas Eve."

David's radio pager went off, sounding a long series of tones. He listened carefully to the dispatch.

"Battalion 10, Medic 21, Medic 22, Engine 21, Engine 22, HazMat 1, Air Ambulance on order. Multi-vehicle accident. Westbound Interstate 80, two miles east of Colfax. Highway Patrol reports several passenger vehicles and a semi with hazardous materials involved."

David grabbed the portable radio from his belt. "Battalion 10 responding." Turning back to Ashley, he shrugged his shoulders. "Gotta go. Give me a hug and keep me posted, okay?"

Ashley wrapped her arms around her friend. "Be safe out there. Thank you from all of us."

"You bet. Anything for you guys." With a wave, he swept out of the room into the hallway, down the stairs, and into the night, emergency lights on and sirens blaring.

Ashley sat at Noah's side in disbelief at how their much-anticipated reunion had ended. Lowering her head, she shut her eyes and prayed for a miracle.

Continue reading for a sample chapter of *Surviving the Firestorm*, book 2 of this series.

BOOK 2

Surviving the Firestorm

Chapter One

Hank slapped his son's backside with a rolled-up newspaper. "Get up, lazy! Make me breakfast. It's Christmas Day."

Jason startled at the rude awakening. "Get your own breakfast." He rolled to his side, pulling up the covers. He had been tossing and turning all night replaying the scene of the accident and had just fallen into a deep sleep.

His dad smacked him harder, this time on the head. "I said get up, now!"

Jason sat up and pushed back the covers and saw the anger in his father's bloodshot eyes. Terrified another beating was imminent, his voice shook with fear. "W-What do you want for breakfast?"

"I don't care. Let's see what we've got. You probably forgot to go to the store, didn't you?" He grabbed the front of Jason's shirt and pulled him closer examining him nose to nose.

Jason cringed at the rank smell of cigarettes and alcohol.

"Hey, what happened to your face?"

Jason shrugged running his tongue over his split lip. He winced as his dad pressed a finger into his swollen nose and black eye. "Just a little scuffle. No big deal."

"It looks like more than a little scuffle. You better put some ice on that…if we have any." He let go of Jason's shirt and jerked his head toward the kitchen. "Get busy. I'm hungry."

Jason walked into the kitchen and found the counters lined with empty whiskey and beer bottles and the sink filled with dirty dishes. Sighing, he started a pot of coffee and peered inside the fridge. "We've got eggs, bread, and orange juice."

"Any bacon or sausage?"

"Nope."

"Then get some today. Make me toast and scrambled eggs," Hank ordered. "I'll have the rest of the juice and a cup of coffee. Make it the way I like it—two teaspoons of sugar and a dash of creamer."

"Ah, we don't have any milk or creamer."

Hank cursed and glared at Jason. "Put that on the list too." He slammed his beefy palm on the kitchen table. "Do I have to think of everything around here?"

"Sorry, Dad. I'll get some today." He poured a mug of coffee and added sugar before sliding it over to his father.

Hank sat down heavily in his recliner and switched on the TV. The news was on with the opening story featuring a hit and run accident with an off-duty fire battalion chief in critical condition.

"Well, that stinks."

Jason looked over his dad's shoulder at the news. Cold dread and a heavy anvil of guilt swept through his body. He hadn't meant to hit anyone, much less a fireman. He'd gotten so distracted by Becka's texts. By the time he realized what had happened, he panicked—and fled. Beads of sweat happened to break out on his forehead. His dad would kill him if he found out. Grateful the man wasn't dead—yet— he pulled out the breakfast ingredients and prepared the food. There were only two eggs and a slice of bread, so he went hungry, as usual. His stomach muscles were so clenched, he couldn't have forced anything down anyway. His hand shook as he set the plate of food and utensils on the kitchen table.

With a grunt, Hank wrestled out of his recliner and walked into the kitchen. He plunked down into his chair at the table and dug into the food. Jason filled the sink with hot water and dish soap. He stood at the sink, scrubbing the same spot on the pan, completely unaware of the passage of time until he heard his dad shove back from the table. He stood, belched, and scratched his belly. After he tossed his dirty plate in the dish water, he took the paper into the living room.

As Jason put the last washed dish in the rack, he heard his dad shouting obscenities. "What happened to my car?"

The front door slammed behind him as he went outside to examine the damage.

"Jason! Get out here. Now!" he thundered.

Jason shook with fear as he followed his dad outside.

The right front bumper was pushed in and smeared with a dark red substance. The right headlight was broken and hanging by a wire. The left one had been burned out for weeks.

"It was really foggy last night."

Hank put both hands on his stocky hips, lips clenched, and face flushed with rage. "So what does that have to do with my car getting messed up?"

Jason clenched his fists nervously. "A... A...deer jumped out in front of me. I... I didn't see it until it hit the car." He swallowed dryly. "I was distracted because Becka broke up with me by text...on Christmas Eve!

Hank stomped over to Jason and shook his finger in his face, then thumped his son's chest hard. "I don't care about your love life! What are you going to do about my car?"

"I'll pay for it to be fixed. I promise."

Hank appraised his son with a critical glare. He analyzed Jason's black eye, swollen nose, and cut lip. "Looks to me like your face connected with the steering wheel. Were you stupid enough not to wear your seat belt?"

Jason hung his head.

"A deer, huh?" He crossed his thick muscular arms and glowered at Jason. "Perhaps it was...a firefighter?"

Jason's heart pulsed with adrenaline. Guilt and fear flooded his body. He knew the damage his dad could do. He'd experienced his rage many times and seen him beat his mother time and time again until she escaped several years ago.

He threw his hands up to protect his face out of habit. Hot tears rolled down his cheeks. "Dad, I swear. It was an accident. A horrible accident. I'm sorry…so sorry." His gangly shoulders and reed-thin body shook. The oppressiveness of guilt shrouded his consciousness. "I'll go to the police and tell them what happened. I'll make it right."

Hank stared in disbelief at his son. "You're such an idiot! Don't you understand? If he dies, you'll be charged with *murder!* You're a minor, but they'll give you time in juvenile hall and then hard time in the slammer." He eyed Jason up and down. "They'll eat your young flesh for breakfast. Believe me. I know firsthand what happens to new meat."

Jason opened his mouth to interject. "But—"

"Shut up. I'm making a plan to save your hide." He looked around furtively to see if anyone was listening. "Get the keys to the car."

Jason questioned him with his eyes.

"Do what I say!"

Jason hustled into the house to grab the car keys while his dad entered the shed next to the house. When he came back outside, his dad was putting gasoline and rags in the trunk.

He gestured to the driver's seat. "Get in."

"What's going on?"

"Shut your piehole! Follow me. Stay right behind." He pulled his helmet on and roared his motorcycle to life.

Jason did as he was told. An hour later, they turned onto a remote logging road. Another half hour passed before they reached their destination: a large circular dirt logging deck free of trees.

"Put the car in the middle of the logging deck, and get the stuff out of the trunk," Hank ordered.

"Are you going to torch the car?" Jason's voice quavered.

"Do you want to end up in jail and me, too, as your accomplice? Don't question me, boy." He handed Jason a pair of surgical gloves and one of the rags. "Wipe anything you could have possibly touched. Steering wheel, dash, everything. Don't forget the inside and outside door handles."

Jason looked at his dad quizzically. "How do you know all this?"

Hank hulked over him, hands fisted. "How do you think I know?" He slapped him on his upper back and pushed him forward. "Do it!"

Jason's heart quaked with fear. *Who was his dad? And what had he done?* He wiped all the prints from the inside of the car and stepped out, carefully wiping the door handles and mirrors.

"Put the other helmet on and get on the bike. I'm going to torch the car, and then we need to get out of here fast. The smoke is going to be big and black. Someone's bound to call it in right away."

Nodding somberly, Jason did what he was told. Hank splashed gasoline inside and outside of the car and saturated the rags. Then he stuffed them into the gas tank.

"Start the bike." He took a lighter out of his pocket and lit the rags.

Flames immediately appeared. He ran over and hopped on the bike with Jason behind him.

"It's going to explode. Hang on!" Revving the engine, he shot out of the loading deck and down the logging trail.

Less than a quarter mile down the road, they could hear the exploding gas tank and feel the ground rumble. Hank wound around the lumber trails, taking a different route before entering the freeway. As they came down the mountain, they could hear the sirens. They pulled to the side of the road to let the fire engines and police pass on their way toward the huge thick black plume of smoke.

"It's going to take a while for those engines to reach the location. I think we're going to be all right." Hank snorted.

Holding his father's waist tightly, Jason lowered his head in shame and defeat.

When they got home, Hank headed for the kitchen to grab a beer. Jason knew better than to remind his dad it was still morning, and Christmas morning for all that mattered. Hank took a big slug of beer and picked up his phone. He punched in three numbers: 9-1-1.

Dispatch immediately answered. "This is 911. State your emergency."

Hank took another swig. "My car was stolen. It was parked out front last night, and now it's gone." Lighting up a cigarette, he grinned and winked at Jason.

ABOUT THE AUTHOR

Inspiring faith, love, and hope, Jen M. Hughes is an author whose novels are geared toward those who enjoy contemporary Christian women's fiction related to first responders.

Website: www.jenmhughes.com.

CPSIA information can be obtained
at www.ICGtesting.com
Printed in the USA
JSHW020839191122
33385JS00002B/10